Bridlington

A Sanford 3rd Age Club Mystery

David W Robinson

in association with Ocelot Press

Ocelot Press

Edited by Maureen Vincent-Northam

Prologue

On a summer's evening, Bridlington North Beach provided a fine view of the North Sea and the green-topped, limestone cliffs of Flamborough Head.

But not at half past nine on a chilly Good Friday in April.

The sun had set more than an hour previously, and half a mile to the south, the town, one of the most popular resorts on the North Yorkshire/Humberside boundary, still thrived in spring revelry, bubbling with the excitement of the Easter weekend just begun.

Climbing out of her car, Detective Inspector Freya Elliman had no mind for the black blanket that was the North Sea or the odd twinkling of distant lights from the minimal maritime traffic. If she had her way, she'd be enjoying an evening out with friends, maybe slaking her thirst with a couple of mojitos, killing off the evening with a vodka kick or two, or at the very worst, slouching in front of the TV and sinking a couple of beers. She could not have her own way. She was duty CID for the holiday weekend, and a body on the beach was her concern.

She parked on the seaward side of Royal Crescent, hit the remote to lock up her car, and walking between two patrol cars, made her way down to the promenade, and from there down onto the sands where her sidekick, Detective Sergeant Tom Buttle stood to one side of the taped off area where the body lay.

When he spotted her, Buttle crushed out his cigarette. 'Evening, boss. Flying start to the Easter weekend, this, innit?'

'The job's the job, Tom. What do you know?'

'Not much. We're still waiting for the doc to turn up. She's a young woman, about thirty-ish. Looks like she was strangled with her scarf. SOCO have had a root through her handbag, and I've got her ID from the driver's licence. Jessica Collier. She's from Sanford, West Yorkshire, which is interesting, because the scarf is in the colours of the Sanford Bulls rugby league team, and they're in town on a weekend thrash.'

Freya sighed. 'All right. Let's have a look at her.'

She lay where she had died, close to the low sea wall, the blue and white, striped scarf still wrapped round her neck. Her mouth was open but her eyes were closed, as if she felt that by closing them she could shut out the reality of her approaching end. Pretty, fashionably dressed, her red hair was in disarray, her hands were clamped on the scarf, and Freya could imagine her fighting to pull the tightening ligature away from her closing airway. Further down, her short skirt had ridden up, baring her chunky thighs, and beneath the hem of the skirt, her plain, white underwear was on view.

'Possible sexual assault?' Freya ventured.

'Not unheard of, ma'am, but I've never come across a nonce who bothered to put her knickers back on after topping her. Thing is, we had a report of a mugging from the International earlier today.'

2

Buttle pointed to the dead woman. 'And she's carrying the bag that was nicked.'

Freya remained noncommittal. 'Let's not jump to conclusions. You say the scarf is to do with the Sanford Bulls and they're in town?'

'They're staying at the International. Some kinda weekend shindig as far as I can gather.' Buttle looked up beyond the promenade and nodded in the direction of a multi-storey, recently constructed hotel.

Freya chewed her lip. 'Is she a fan, or part of the club? Or is it the earlier victim taking revenge?' She pulled herself together. 'Let's get up there and see who knows whatever.'

Chapter One

Seven weeks previously, early in the evening of the last Wednesday in February, the top room of the Miners Arms was ready for the weekly meeting and disco of the Sanford 3rd Age Club.

Alone in the room, the club's management trio, Joe Murray, Sheila Riley, and an ailing Brenda Jump, were in the middle of a flustered debate.

Joe cast a mildly irritated, bewildered glance at Brenda, shook his head, and declared, 'I can't believe I'm hearing this.'

Brenda, her face pale, eyes sad, tried to protest. 'Joe, I understand what—'

He interrupted her. 'Sheila and I agreed on this, Brenda. It's for your benefit. You've been through hell, and you don't need to be freezing your tribbles off on Flamborough Head. You need the sun, sand, and se… silliness of the Costa Blanca.'

'Joe—'

'Brenda—'

At this point, Sheila Riley cut him off. 'Joe, you're getting out of your pram. Let's listen to what Brenda has to say.' She glanced at her watch. 'It's turned half past seven. The members will be arriving any time now. We have to present a united front, and we can't do that if we're arguing between ourselves.'

Joe gave up the argument. 'All right. I'm listening.'

Brenda took their hands. 'I owe you my life.

Both of you. If it hadn't been for you two, that evil…' She heaved in a shuddering breath. 'I swear she'd have left me there to starve to death. She even said so, if you remember.'

Four days previously, late on Saturday night, she was freed after being abducted and spending a full week bound to a wooden dining chair, incarcerated in a dark, defunct, military installation. Joe, charged with delivering the ransom, had confronted her abductor, who was subsequently arrested, charged, and remanded for trial. Once freed, Brenda was shipped to Sanford General Hospital. Discharged on the Monday morning, she was temporarily rooming with Sheila and beginning the slow journey to full recovery. Still in shock, still weak through a lack of nutrition, still suffering from exposure, prone to breaking down crying, she remained a shadow of the lusty, full of life woman everyone knew.

During the frantic days of her absence, when the only contact was through her captor's video messages, Joe and Sheila privately decided that once the ordeal was over, Brenda would need regeneration in the shape of a week in Benidorm, a lively, fun loving Spanish resort, perfect for a lively, fun loving Yorkshire woman.

If there was a problem, it harked back to a general meeting of the Sanford 3rd Age Club at the beginning of the year when the members decided that their first spring outing would be to Bridlington for the Easter weekend. In the aftermath of Brenda's abduction, Joe insisted that he would change the members' minds but Brenda did not want to hear it.

5

Her voice a distant echo of its normal exuberance, she cast a tearful gaze upon her two best friends. 'We run the club for the members, not for ourselves, not for our own wants or needs. They decided on Bridlington in January, and it's less than eight weeks away. You can't change it now, Joe. Besides, I don't know that I'll be able to cope with the hassle of airports, flights, transfers from Alicante and all the rest of it. Please, Joe, please leave it as it is. Let's have a weekend in Bridlington, and then maybe we can think about Benidorm later in the year. When I'm better.'

Joe squeezed her hand, and looked to Sheila for guidance.

'Brenda is right. Not everyone is flush with money, Joe, and some of our less well-off members would struggle to afford Benidorm. We promised them a weekend away. Let's stick to the original plans and rather than insisting we change it, propose Benidorm for, say, September or October. Give people time to sort out whether they can afford it or whether they want to go.'

He shrugged. 'We three have been the backbone of this club since forever. Hell, it was our idea. A club for middle agers like us. No bloody kids, no rotten twentysomethings, no gadabout hipsters.' He pointed a bony finger Brenda. 'I don't know how much work this woman has done for them over the years but the least they could do is consider paying some of it back by helping her recover from what that swine did to her.'

Brenda tried a weak smile. 'If I didn't know you better, Joe Murray, I'd swear blind you really

6

cared.' She reached up, pulled him down close to her face, and kissed him on the cheek. 'Bridlington, Joe. Please.'

He tutted. 'You give in too easy, you do.'

Sheila's lips pursed. 'If the whispers are anything to go by, she's spent a good few years giving in too easily to you.'

Having got her way, Brenda changed the subject. 'Have you booked the hotel, Joe?'

'As it happens, no. I was supposed to do it last week, but you went missing and I never got round to it. Not to worry. It'll be an Accomplus place, and they make so much money out of us, they'll fit us in at a discounted price. Don't you worry about it.'

'It's Easter weekend,' Sheila reminded them. 'I hope they have plenty of vacancies.'

'Trust me, I'll get it sorted.'

The members began to file in, a trickle at first, slowly increasing until, with the clock reading just a few minutes to eight, the room was full. As club secretary, Sheila prepared to take the minutes, and Joe stood before the assembly to formally open the meeting.

'Good evening, everyone. Before we go any further, I'm sure we'd all like to celebrate the safe return of our close and trusted friend, our treasurer, Brenda Jump.'

A spontaneous round of applause broke out causing Brenda to blush, and then prompting the free flow of tears. It was entirely in keeping with the membership that they would support any individual suffering the after-effects of even trivial trauma, let alone the criminal abuse to which Brenda had been

7

subjected.

As the applause settled, Joe expanded on his initial announcement. 'The ratbag concerned is locked up, and awaiting trial. While we're on the subject, I have some additional thanks to share with you. Every one of you demonstrated the solidarity of our little club, but in particular, Les Tanner, George Robson, Owen Frickley, and of course, your secretary, Sheila Riley, all assisted in bringing the matter to a safe and successful conclusion. Thank you, gentlemen, and er, lady.'

Led by Joe, another smattering of applause carried around the room accompanied by murmurs of approval.

As it died down, Joe took the microphone again. 'Now on this subject, I was going to propose a change of plan. I believe that Brenda is in need of some serious sunshine and rest and recuperation, so I was going to ask you to forget Bridlington and focus on Benidorm.' The muttering this time was one of consternation but Joe pressed on before any complaints could be raised. 'I've already been told to shut my trap, and it was Brenda who told me to shut it.'

'Hear, hear,' Alec Staines called out, and was greeted with a ripple of laughter.

Joe narrowed a glower on the Staines couple. 'You should be more generous to me, Alec, especially if you want the contract for repainting the kitchen of The Lazy Luncheonette.' He paused to allow another room-wide chuckle. 'So, folks, Bridlington it is. I haven't booked the hotel yet, but I'll be on with it first thing tomorrow, so before we wrap up this evening, I'll want all names to Sheila…'

An hour later, the formal part of the evening dealt with, the disco in full flow, Joe cried off for a few minutes and made his way out to the car park for a smoke.

He was still slightly irked that it would be Yorkshire not the Costa Blanca, and it wasn't all to do with Brenda's trauma.

He had suffered from gastric problems for over a year, brought to a head by Sheila and Brenda during the Meddlercon visit when Brenda suggested it might be colorectal cancer. From there Joe had pressed his GP and the local hospital for further investigation. He had already had a couple of polyps removed, but that had not cleared up the problem. After the removal of a third polyp, described as sessile, the kind which could lead to cancer, the surgeon had told him he was probably suffering from diverticulosis but that had never been confirmed, and his GP prescribed the appropriate medication, which included strong painkillers and muscle relaxants.

To Joe (and his friends) it came as something of a relief. Provided he was careful, if he had no fever, if he was not suffering diarrhoea or vomiting, he was not barred from working behind the counter and in the kitchen of his café, but it did him few favours when the pain came to bite at him.

He put his problems aside when Brenda was abducted, but now that she was safely back with them, albeit still in a weak and distressed state, he got to thinking about his own health. A week in

Benidorm might just help his tummy troubles more than a weekend in Bridlington. There again, it might not, but at least he would be suffering in more clement weather. Selfish, yes, but with Brenda now safe, he could afford to be.

'Now then, you old git. How are you keeping?'

Immersed in his ruminations, Joe took a moment to realise that the voice was speaking to him. He looked round into the smiling face of Hayden Ollister, Chair of the Sanford Bulls Rugby League club.

Joe smiled and turned to shake hands. 'Good to see you, Ollie. And you're looking well.'

Like many people born in Sanford during the 1960s, Ollister detested his given name. Joe numbered himself amongst such people. He hated his full name, Joseph, but shortening it to Joe was acceptable. His brother, Arthur, felt the same way and since his move to Australia, he had insisted friends address him as Art. It was difficult to see how Hayden could be curtailed, unless it was to Hay or Hen, neither of which appealed, so he insisted that people called him Ollie.

About Joe's age (56) a useful full back in his playing days, he held a similar position to Joe in that he ran his own, successful business. Construction rather than catering, but he never seemed to be short of work and if Joe's estimate was on the mark, he wasn't short of money either. As chairman of the Sanford Bulls, he was the man largely responsible for the running of the club as a sporting entity, the same capacity Joe filled for the Sanford 3rd Age Club, although the latter could hardly be described as sporting. On the other hand, when Joe considered the antics of members such as George Robson and Owen Frickley, sporting was perhaps appropriate.

Ollister still exhibited a tall and broad figure, his six foot, muscular frame dwarfing Joe's rake-thin, five and a half feet. But Ollister's head of dark hair had thinned and was in the process of turning a gentlemanly grey, and Joe sensed a slight tiredness about him. Only to be expected when Joe considered the man's age and the responsibility he shouldered: running a thriving business and running the rugby club.

Dropping his car keys in his pocket, Ollister dug out his pipe. 'I thought you and your lot had a meeting tonight, Joe.'

Joe aimed a finger at the upper floor of the pub. 'Over and done with, Ollie. Disco's on and I sneaked out for a quick cough and spit.' His craggy features sagged. 'You, er, you know what happened to Brenda?'

Ollie nodded. 'Doesn't everyone in Sanford? How is she?'

'Bad. Who wouldn't be?'

'Whisper is you've not been too well this last year or more, too.'

'Gar. Summat and nowt, mate. They've had a look at my insides—'

Ollie cut in. 'Camera down the throat... Or...' he trailed off and looked down at Joe's midriff.

'Yes. It was "*or*".' Joe chuckled. 'Anyway, getting back to Brenda, she'll need a fair lot of TLC over the coming weeks, mate. Anyway, everyone voted for a weekend in Bridlington at the start of the year. I thought Brenda needed summat better so I suggested Benidorm, but I got voted down before I could even put it forward. Bridlington it is. I've left Sheila getting the names.'

Ollister laughed. 'You never did like losing, did you? Shame you weren't bigger. We might have signed you on.'

Joe laughed too. 'I can't see you having much use for a prop who's only five foot five and weighs less than eight stones. So, how are you?'

Ollister's face fell. 'In the wars, mate. On two fronts.'

'Try talking to me about it. They say it helps, you know, when you talk about your troubles.'

The other laughed, a short, sardonic bark. 'You're just a nosy bugger.'

'True, but don't let that stop you.'

Ollister lit his pipe and sucked on it. An action which Joe recognised as a ploy designed to help the man gather his thoughts.

'You might have missed this because of all the hoo-hah over Brenda, but we had a break in at the club last week. Trophy cabinet smashed and half a dozen cups stolen. Whoever it was also smashed up the security cameras and would you believe it, they wiped the recordings. All up, the damage comes to two or three grand.'

Joe sympathised. 'Hell's bells. You'll be well insured though.'

'We are, but that's not the point, Joe. Some of those trophies go back years, and from a sentimental point of view, they're irreplaceable. Pity you're not still working as a private eye or I'd have hired you.'

'I am still working as a private eye,' Joe assured him, 'but that's not the kind of case I take on. And is that it, Ollie? All that's bothering you, is it? Or is there more?'

Ollister sucked on the pipe again and blew a cloud of smoke into the dark, cold night. 'No. You're right, Joe. Fact is, Joe, I'm about to become a grandad.'

'That's a cause for celebration, surely?' Joe pursed his lips to show that he was impressed. 'It'll be that girl of yours? Matilda, is it?'

'You mean, Tilly.' Ollister's lips spread in a thin, sad smile. 'She's like me, you know. She hates her given name, but I never had no say in the matter. Anyway, she insists we call her Tilly. We tried Matty, but she said it made her sound like a coat of paint. She's married to Dave Drummond, you know.'

Taking a drag on his hand-rolled cigarette, Joe frowned. 'Dave Drummond? Do I know him? I remember Paul Drummond, Rott, as we used to call him. Attitude like a Rottweiler, and a temper to match.'

'Aye, well, Dave is Rott's younger brother. Big bugger, just like Rott, but better tempered and more focused on the game. Rott was too fond of his beer.'

Joe found the discussion preferable to arguments over 3rd Age Club outings. 'We were at young Wes Staines's wedding in the Lake District a while back, you know. That's the last time we saw Rott or Wes. Doing well for themselves up there, you know. Plumbing and electrics, making more

13

than a sausage butty out of the job.'

'They were a hell of a trio, you know,' Ollister said. 'Young Staines, Rott, and your Lee. Put the fear of God into the opposition every time they played. Shame Lee's knee got smashed up. You weren't there for that match, were you? It was deliberate, you know. That opposition full back deliberately kicked him in the kneecap. Your Lee was in agony, but it didn't stop him getting up and wrapping his hands round the other bloke's throat. If we hadn't dragged him off, he'd have murdered the guy.'

'Out of character, too,' Joe said. 'For all his size, Lee's an even tempered lad. Never loses it.' He stubbed out his cigarette. 'So, go on. You're about to become a grandad. Why so glum?'

'Tilly and Dave. They're in the middle of World War Three. You see, Joe, they're only young, and with Tilly so close to her date – she's due sometime around Easter – Dave's not getting enough how's your father, and Tilly says he's playing away from home. I find it hard to believe, but she's absolutely certain of it.' Ollister stared Joe in the eye. 'What do you do with that kind of situation?'

Joe shrugged again. 'Haven't a clue. Me and Alison never had kids. Fact is, Lee's the closest I have to a son. All I can say, Ollie, is stand by your daughter. She's blood. Dave Drummond's only an in-law.'

Ollister's pipe had gone out. He put a light to it and abruptly changed the subject. 'So you're going to Bridlington are you?'

14

'Easter weekend.'

'Aye, well, that reminds me. We had a match in York back in October, and as a treat, I booked the lads into a hotel. I meanersay, it's close enough to have driven over, played the match, and come home in the day, but we were giving the team a bit of party time. Anyway, we stayed overnight at the Palmer. Part of the Accomplus group. As we were signing in, I got talking to the manageress. Smart looking woman, mid-forties, blonde, and she told me that she knows you well.'

A broad smile crossed Joe's cragged features. 'Yvonne Vallance. I'll bet she's still with her husband, though.'

Ollister laughed aloud. 'Why? What makes you think you'd have a chance with her? And yes, we did meet her husband. Geoff, his name is. Tall. A bit younger than her, and she told me you had something to do with them coming together.'

Joe chuckled at the memory. 'Nah, not really. It's a year or two back now, but we were staying at the Palmer over Halloween. It was when that MP, Edgar Prudhoe, was murdered. Anyway, she has this mangled hand—'

'I noticed. One of the fingers missing. Summat to do with dragging her first husband out of a burning building.'

'That's the woman. She was self-conscious about it and Geoff fancied her rotten, but he let the hand put him off. I told her to stop living in the past, deal with her disability, and I told him to forget about the hand, and whisk her off to his bed. Next thing I heard, they were married.' Joe's features fell.

15

'Yes, and I didn't even get an invite.'

Ollister laughed yet again. 'Joe Murray, matchmaker. Doesn't gel, somehow.'

Joe dragged on his cigarette again and shivered in the wintery chill. 'So what does this have to do with Bridlington?'

'Well, we got nattering and she was telling me as how Accomplus have opened up a new hotel in Bridlington. The International. Classy place near the seafront somewhere. Her sister-in-law's running it. Reckoned if we booked there we'd get a loyalty discount, and as it happens we have a match over there at Easter. Give her a bell and maybe you'll get a good few quid off the price for you and your crowd, and you never know, we might see you there.'

'Interesting. Thanks for that, Ollie. I reckon we might just be staying at the…what was it again? The International?'

Chapter Two

As always, Joe and his nephew, Lee, opened up The Lazy Luncheonette as usual at six the following morning.

Twenty-eight-year-old Lee, a former prop with the Sanford Bulls rugby league team before his knee was smashed, was a giant of a man. Tall, muscular, a man who kept himself in the peak of physical fitness, yet possessed of a sometimes slow and simple mind which tended to see everything in black and white. He and his wife, Cheryl, were permanent assistants in the café, and it had to be said that Lee was an excellent cook, one who was more capable than the everyday, simple meals he was asked to prepare.

'Did you have a good meeting last night, Uncle Joe?' Lee asked as they prepared to open.

'We did not,' Joe snapped. Everyone was used to his irritability at this hour of the day, and Lee took little notice. 'I got voted down. We're going to Bridling-sodding-ton instead of Beni-bloody-dorm for Easter.'

Lee laughed. 'That'll go down well with our Cheryl. She'll want us to come over with our Danny on the Saturday after we shut The Lazy Luncheonette and we'll happen stay for the Sunday an'all.'

Joe nodded. 'Well, when she's made her mind up, let me know. I'll book and pay for a room for you.' He dug into his pockets. 'Get the hobs and hotplates up and running. I'll just stand outside the back door and have a quick cough.'

He moved to the rear of the kitchen, thrust the door open, quickly rolled a cigarette, lit it and suffered the inevitable coughing fit, which he relieved with an intake of salbutamol from an inhaler.

The sun would not rise for almost an hour and he stared out over the dark spread of Sanford Retail Park. Some of the day's customers would come from there, but that did not interest him. Instead, the night view fitted with his mood, a symptom, he diagnosed, of the past week or more and the trauma of Brenda's abduction. Everyone understood that the woman herself would need time to get over it properly, but he reasoned that the same applied to himself and Sheila, Brenda's two closest friends. Fifty years or more they had known each other, and notwithstanding marriages and the end of same (widowhood for the two women, divorce for Joe) nothing had ever come between the three. Occasional arguments, true, rare, more serious fallouts, but nothing, absolutely nothing would ever threaten that alliance. The downside of that was when one or other of them ran into serious problems. Then, all three would suffer.

Sheila arrived at seven o'clock, and as she changed into her tabard, ready for the morning crush, Joe remonstrated with her. 'You're supposed to be looking after Brenda. You didn't have to come in.'

'Wrong,' Sheila disagreed. 'There's nothing wrong with me that work won't put right.'

18

'Yeah, but what about Brenda? Is she ready to be left alone?'

Sheila did not hesitate. 'She and I talked about this last night, Joe. Somewhere along the line, she has to get used to being alone again. Good Lord, we're both widows, we're both accustomed to the solitary life, and she has to get back into that frame of mind. She won't do it with me fussing over her like a mother hen. She was still in bed when I left, and she probably won't get up until, perhaps eight o'clock. By then it'll be broad daylight. She says she'll stay in the house and keep the doors locked, and she won't answer the door to anyone.' She sighed. 'I think she's fine, physically. It's the psychological impact that she has to get over.'

Joe nodded his agreement. 'Not just her. I was thinking about it while I had a smoke at the back door. What kind of effect will it have on all of us? Crikey, Sheila, we're her best friends, and when you think about it, what happened to her could have happened to us.' He felt his temper spooling up. 'I should have kicked that cow's bloody head in when she was on the deck.'

'And spent the next however many years in jail? I don't think so. Now, shall we get on with some work before the draymen arrive?'

The draymen of Sanford Brewery had been stalwart customers of The Lazy Luncheonette for over half a century, ever since Joe's father set it up as Alf's Cafe. There were other small eateries in and around Sanford, but they had always preferred the food at Joe's place. Not only the food. They enjoyed nothing more than winding Joe up, and never a man to back down, Joe gave as good as he got.

Within twenty minutes, those same draymen began to turn up, and by half past seven, the queue stretched from the counter to the front entrance and beyond.

Barry Standish, one of Joe's main antagonists, was instrumental in marshalling the draymen during Brenda's abduction, all but ordering his colleagues to keep their eyes open for any sign of the woman, and every day during that week, he had demanded progress reports. Now that the episode was over and done with, his concern did not relent.

After ordering a full English breakfast with toast, he asked, 'How's Brenda?'

'Getting there, Barry. Slow but sure. It'll take time.'

'Well, make sure you tell her that me and the boys are asking after her.' Having done what he considered his duty, Barry switched modes. 'What's this I hear about you lot shooting off to Bridlington for Easter?'

Joe tutted and pushed a beaker of tea across the counter to Barry. 'It's a good job the 3rd Age Club meetings aren't part of MI5. We only made the final decision last night so how come you know about it?'

'Word gets around, Joe. Your gang of thugs can't keep their traps shut.' Barry laughed. 'I bumped into George Robson and Owen Frickley in the Foundry Inn late last night. I think they were looking for a lock in. So it's definitely Bridlington, is it?'

'Yep.' Joe held out his hand for the money and Barry handed over a tenner. 'So where are you going for Easter?'

'Nowhere. Busy time for us, Joe, and we can't get the time off. Me and the missus are going to Lanzarote for the May bank holiday weekend.'

Joe rang up the sale, dropped the note in the till, gathered change, checked it and handed it over. 'Lanzarote? Not bad, but I have to say, I prefer Tenerife.'

Barry laughed. 'So your underpants can hang on the line with your ex-wife's knickers? You're a sly one, Joe Murray.'

The draymen were away and about their day's work by half past eight, and the clerks and admins of the offices above and around the café took over to complete the morning's rush. Their orders were different to the brewery employees. More eclectic, more exotic (in Joe's opinion) and by coincidence, more profitable.

By half past nine, the morning rush was complete, and Joe excused himself, made his way out to his car, took out his smartphone and after checking the directory entries, punched the dialling icon.

'Good morning, Palmer Hotel, Yvonne speaking.'

Joe put a smile in his voice. 'Guess who.'

'Joe Murray, as I live and breathe. So what can I do for you this morning, you old toe rag?'

'Plenty, but you'd need to get rid of Geoff for a few hours.'

Yvonne laughed. 'That could be difficult, and even if I could, what do you have that Daniel Craig and Pierce Brosnan don't have more of?'

21

'Yorkshire staying power. Need I say more?'

She chuckled again. 'Nuff said. Now come on, Joe, what do you want nagging me at this time of a busy morning? Are you bringing your gang of thugs here again, or is it just you and your latest girlfriend for a naughty weekend?'

'Neither. It's something that was said to me last night. The club are going to Bridlington for the Easter weekend, and a friend of mine hinted that your sister is running an Accomplus place there.'

'Sister-in-law,' Yvonne corrected him. 'Natalie. Geoff's sister, and yes, she's in charge at the International. It's about half a mile out of Bridlington centre.'

'Great. Well—'

She interrupted. 'You want me to put in a word for you and your people, make sure you get a decent discount?'

Now Joe laughed heartily. 'You know me too well.'

'Your staying power is all about your wallet. Leave it with me, Joe, and I'll have a word with Natalie. You don't mind if I give her your number?'

'Course not. And I'll wait to hear from her. And thanks, Yvonne. If you can think of any way I can *really* thank you, don't hesitate to let me know.'

Perfectly accustomed to his innuendo, Yvonne insisted, 'The best way you can thank me is to book your people here for a few days.'

'Later in the year,' Joe promised. 'I'll see what I can do.'

He ended the call, climbed out of the car, locked it up and was about to return to the café when

22

the phone tweeted to indicate an incoming text message.

One of his biggest irritations was people obsessed with their mobile phones. They never seemed to be off them, the phone either glued to their ears or in their hands reading, replying to text messages. And yet it never occurred to him that he might be straying along the same route. He accessed the text messages, opened it, and stared in disbelief.

It isn't over yet.

What wasn't over yet?

Over the years of "poking his nose in" he had made any number of enemies. Many of them had been discussed during Brenda's abduction, and the majority of them were still in prison. But that by no means applied to all of them and this message from a source he did not recognise, read like a threat.

Or was it just his suspicious mind?

For his sins, he was well-known throughout Sanford, and there were many factors which contributed to that "fame", not least of which was his habit of complaining about the local borough council's alleged inefficiency and expense, and it was entirely possible that this kind of message could have come from someone at the town hall. Right away, he dismissed Les Tanner. Anything the former TAVR captain had to say he would say face-to-face, not via a text message from an unregistered mobile phone. But Les wasn't the only council employee Joe had upset down the years, although for the life of him, he couldn't remember any particular incidents in recent months, nor could he think of anything that was ongoing.

He made his way back into the café, relieved Sheila at the checkout, allowing her to assist Kayleigh in delivering orders and clearing tables, and handed his phone to Cheryl, his nephew's wife.

'Take a look at that latest text message, lass. How do I go about tracking down the call?'

Like many young people, her fingers danced over the screen in a way Joe and his middle-aged friends could not emulate. She read the message, checked the potential source, then shut the phone down and handed it back. 'You can't. You'd need specialised tackle like what the police have, and even then all you'd get back would be whatever false name the sender's using. What does it mean it, it isn't over yet?'

Joe dropped the phone in his pocket. 'Ask me another.'

'It'll probably be one of his hidden girlfriends insisting that she wants more out of his wallet,' Sheila said as she returned to the counter.

'Ha-bloody-ha,' Joe said and focused on his next customer, a woman looking for tea, and toast.

At 10:30, he took a break with Sheila at table 5, the one they always used. With the Daily Express opened at the crossword page, he focused on it. Opposite him, Sheila was reading a magazine. The silence between them was contemplative not bitter. Neither of them had anything to say.

And then, without warning, Joe's phone rang. Sheila was on immediate alert. 'Brenda?'

He studied the menu screen, and shook his head. 'I know her number, and I know yours, but the phone doesn't know this one.' The curious text message at the forefront of his mind, he made the connection, put the phone to his ear. 'Joe Murray.'

'Oh. Right. Am I speaking to *the* Joe Murray? The one my sister-in-law says is a legend?'

Ever since that Halloween weekend at the Palmer, Yvonne had become a good friend of the Sanford 3rd Age Club's management triumvirate, and Joe played upon it by putting a smile in his voice. 'A lot of people think I'm more of a leg end. Is this Natalie at the International in Bridlington? Geoff Vallance is your brother?'

'It is. And to be frank, Mr Murray, I wouldn't think of making a call like this, but Yvonne speaks very highly of you.'

'First, please call me Joe. Next, to be brutally honest, I think Yvonne only married your brother because she knew I was unavailable.'

'To be equally honest, Joe, she did say something about the way Brad Pitt and Russell Crowe weren't available at the time, so she had to settle for our Geoff.'

He laughed. 'She's obsessed with movie glitz. Now, Natalie, let's get down to business. I was talking to a friend of mine last night. Hayden Ollister, Chair of the Sanford Bulls rugby team. He stayed at the Palmer a while back, and it was him that put me on to you.'

'Yvonne told me the tale, and you're looking for a block booking over Easter weekend. Yes?'

'Correct. Ollie recommended your place, and right away, I thought, if the woman of my dreams has a sister-in-law on the coast, it's my duty to make myself known to you.'

25

'And I'm seriously happy to hear from you. Now come on, Joe. I'm a busy woman, so what is it you want?'

'Accommodation for the Sanford 3rd Age Club from April eighteenth – that's Good Friday – to Monday – Easter Monday, obviously – the twenty-first. Can you do it… at a decent discount?'

'Tsk. Why are you men all alike? Always demanding.' She became more businesslike. 'Right, Joe, you know the script with Accomplus. For a decent sized booking, I can give you five percent to start, but more than that depends on numbers. Bring me a full bus load and I should be able to up the discount to ten percent or maybe more.' She paused, covering the mouthpiece to deal with a guest. A minute later she came back. 'Sorry about that. Now, do we have a deal?'

'That sounds ideal.'

'How soon can you confirm?'

'I should have a full passenger list in, say, two days. The minute I get it, I'll email it to you, and you can give me the final price. Okay?'

'Perfect. And I'll look forward to seeing you on Good Friday.'

Joe killed the call, dropped the phone in his pocket, and smiled across the table at Sheila. 'All done and dusted. We'll be digging in at the International, Bridlington over Easter.'

Sheila returned his pleasant smile. 'Thank God for that. I know you wanted Benidorm, Joe, but I really think Bridlington will be better for Brenda.'

'Yeah, you may be right. And let's look on the positive side. Both places begin with the letter B.'

26

Chapter Three

February turned to March and by the middle of a sunny, but bitterly cold month, Brenda made a tearful return to work. They were tears of gratitude at the unashamed love and concern shown by Lee, Cheryl, and Kayleigh, augmented by the arrival of the draymen who took turns to ask after her health and express their pleasure at seeing her back.

The woman herself was much improved, but while she was reluctant to be left alone, she had moved back to her own home and dragooned Joe and Sheila to help her spring clean the place.

It was during that period when Joe received another text message.

Worried are you? You should be.

It irritated him to the point, where he replied by text. *I don't know who you are, but go to hell. Better yet, come and face me and I'll send you there.*

Cheryl took him to task. 'You never reply to these people, Joe. Do that and you're playing their game. In fact you should take it to the cops.'

'Yeah, and I can just see how our Gemma would react. You think I'm a grouch but she's way ahead of me when she's got it on her.'

As it would turn out, Joe was nearer the mark. He would receive no more messages in March.

By the time April appeared on the calendar, Brenda was more like her old self: energetic, enthusiastic, fun-loving. She was particularly grateful to Joe who had been on point the night she was rescued, and her appreciation of his efforts caused Cheryl to ask of Sheila, 'Is she thanking him in her own special way?'

Brenda's best friend frowned. 'According to my guess, she's thanked him every night of this last week. I don't know where she gets the energy.'

Cheryl tutted. 'Or the inclination.'

Despite the improvement in her outgoing personality, it was noticeable that she never wanted to be alone. She would not even take on the job of delivering the sandwich order to Ingleton Engineering, a mile or so down the road from The Lazy Luncheonette.

'You do the job in broad daylight, dear,' Sheila had reminded her. 'And you're in a car.'

'Yes, I know, but I have to get out of the car at the other end, and again when I get back here. You never know who might be hanging about.'

Even though she had left Sheila's place and moved back to her own home, it was noticeable that at the end of every day she ensured she got home in daylight, careful to ensure no one was anywhere near before she climbed out of her car, and the moment she entered the house, she locked and bolted all the doors and would not answer them to anyone. On the other hand, as Sheila hinted, she was happy to spend many nights with Joe. Not as frequently as her best friend suggested, but more often than would be considered normal.

Joe refused to be drawn on the number of times he and Brenda spent the night together. It was no one's business but theirs, he insisted when asked. But he did spread his concern to friends and the café's crew, especially when they suggested counselling.

'She needs time, not some airhead telling her to grow up.'

'Counselling doesn't work like that, Joe,' Sheila insisted. 'You should know. You saw a counsellor when you tried to give up smoking.'

'I did, and he was less use than a chocolate teapot. At least, I could have eaten the chocolate.'

As if backing Joe, Brenda steadfastly refused to see any counsellor or therapist, relying instead on her friends and colleagues, but amongst them only Joe knew the absolute truth. Even during the time she stayed with Sheila, her best friend remained unaware of the night terrors, when Brenda would wake, trembling, bathed in sweat, weeping to herself, sometimes, cowering in a corner, hiding from a non-existent threat.

By the time Good Friday appeared on the calendar, she was much improved, but still had some way to go and insisted that the imminent weekend in Bridlington would infuse her with the final drops of energy and enthusiasm she needed to overcome the frightening memories. Joe and Sheila applauded her determined attitude.

'And I suppose I'll be the one carrying your shopping for you,' Joe quipped.

Kayleigh frowned. 'Why will you be carrying their shopping, Uncle Joe?' Despite not being a relative, she always referred to him as "Uncle Joe" as a mark of respect.

'Because that's the only reason they ever take me on the Sanford 3rd Age Club outings. A pack mule.'

Brenda gave him a mock sweet smile. 'I've got your harness polished already.'

At just after nine a.m. on that nippy, overcast Friday morning, with all this at the forefront of his mind, Joe, Sheila and Brenda were preparing to leave for the coast.

Even though the early rush (generated, as always, by the Sanford Brewery draymen) was over, The Lazy Luncheonette was still busy. Office workers from the companies above and around them, early shoppers making for Sanford Retail Park, late staff making for their employment on Sanford Retail Park.

Easter bunnies and fake chocolate eggs were carefully placed around the café, and soft, pleasant, instrumental music permeated the dining area, augmented by the wall-mounted television showing cartoon channels, the whole creating an ambience which found favour with everyone, staff and customers alike... with the exception of Joe.

'You don't like it because we thought of it, Sheila and me, not you,' Cheryl told him.

'Wrong,' Joe retorted. 'I don't like it because that CD player uses electricity and we have to pay for it.'

'Tightwad.'

'Granted.'

The coach would leave the Miners Arms at ten, and under normal circumstances Sheila and Brenda would not be at work, but taking into account the anticipated level of business and Brenda's reluctance to be alone, the two women had agreed to come in early and deal with the breakfast rush, on the understanding that at half past nine, all three would make their way to the Miners Arms, half a mile along Doncaster Road, to join their fellow members and board the bus for the coast and the coming weekend.

Back in February, less than forty-eight hours after receiving the full passenger list of 70 members from Sheila, he scanned it and emailed it to Yvonne at the International in return for which he received an better than adequate discount on the overall price.

After the death of his partner, Denise Latham, and thanks to his current health issues Joe had become a different man; freer, more than ready to take a few days off from the café which had been his life for all his life. Notwithstanding Brenda's issues and the need to get away from Sanford if only for a few days, as the weeks progressed he became edgier, more concerned about leaving the business during what would likely be a busy period.

Staff levels were not an issue. Lee, Cheryl, and Kayleigh, were permanent, and they could call upon sufficient, casual support from friends and relatives. They were reliable, they knew what they were doing, and they had never yet let the side down. It was the attraction of work after a year on and off the sick list, exacerbated by the very thought of leaving the place to his nephew at such a busy time which troubled Joe.

'How many times do we have to say that we've done it before,' Sheila pointed out. 'Any number of times. They've never burned the place down.'

31

'Yes they have,' Joe argued. 'That time we were in Blackpool at Easter.'

'It wasn't them who set fire to the old building, Joe,' Brenda reminded him. 'Now stop being a pain in the posterior. We're going to Bridlington and that's that.'

Even now, with their departure less than an hour away, Joe's anxiety had not quite settled, and he spent much of the morning, between serving customers, reminding Cheryl of this, that, those, them, until it reached the point where she ordered. 'For crying out loud, shut it, Joe. We know what we're doing. Now clear off to Brid' and leave us all in peace.'

The comment was greeted with a barely muted chorus of "well said" from the queue waiting for service.

'And don't forget,' Cheryl told him, 'Me and Lee are bring Danny over tomorrow afternoon.'

'As if you'd ever let me forget,' Joe grumbled. Aloud he said, 'Your room's booked and paid for.'

Cheryl softened her attitude. 'Thanks, Joe. You know we love you really.'

'Then why do I sometimes get the impression that you love me with the same passion you reserve for toothache?'

'It's because you're as annoying as toothache,' Brenda told him as she passed into the kitchen.

After serving two office women with coffee to take away, Joe managed to find a few minutes to himself, and he used them to study the passenger list. It was then that he noticed a name which filled him with fresh irritation.

32

'Who the hell invited Angela Foster?'

It brought an impatient cluck from Sheila and another chuckle from Brenda. An encouraging sign in Joe's opinion.

'Angela is a member, Joe,' Sheila pointed out. 'She's perfectly entitled to be with us.'

Brenda threw in her twopence worth. 'We're away in just over half an hour and you've only just noticed she's on the list. How come you didn't twig it when you read it to the woman at the hotel?'

'Because I didn't read it,' he retorted. 'I emailed it. And before you ask, no, I didn't read it beforehand.'

A sly smile crossed Brenda's lips. 'You mean you were so busy chatting up Yvonne Vallance's sister-in-law, you couldn't be bothered. As if the poor woman would look twice at a cranky old sod like you.'

Joe replied with a smile. That was more like the old Brenda.

Alongside them, Kayleigh commented, 'I didn't think Uncle Joe was a Canasova.'

'Joe? A Casanova?' Sheila said. 'The truth is, Kayleigh, he has a thing about Yvonne Vallance, but she also has a thing and it's called Geoff, her husband. He's twice the size of Joe, and if he tried his luck with Yvonne, there'd be a genuine ghost in the old inn at the Palmer. Joe's ghost.'

The man himself bristled. 'Yes, well, after inviting Angela Foster, it's more likely that it'll be her ghost haunting the place in Bridlington. I mean, who let her join the club in the first place. It had to be one of you two cos I know I didn't.'

'It was neither of us, Joe,' Sheila said. 'She joined back in the days when Les Tanner was Chair.'

'Typical,' Joe fumed. 'Bloody typical. Tanner couldn't organise the proverbial in a brewery.' He rounded on the two women. 'And you didn't stop him?'

'There's nothing wrong with Angela,' Brenda insisted. 'She's quite a likeable woman.'

'Likeable? Have you forgotten what she did to me?'

Carrying a bread tray full of dirty dishes back to the kitchen, Kayleigh, paused again. 'Ooh. What did she do, Uncle Joe?'

Sheila answered before he could. 'Angela runs the Sanford Dating Agency, and she wouldn't have Joe as a member. She said he was too grumpy.'

'Can you imagine that?' Joe protested. 'Grumpy? Me?'

Sheila chuckled and went on to explain to Kayleigh, 'It was during the Sanford Valentine Strangler affair. One of Joe's girlfriends was a victim and Joe was a suspect for a short time.'

'Yes, and when she wouldn't have me as a member of her dating agency, I told her it would be a cold day in hell before I'd let her into the 3rd Age Club.'

Brenda laughed again. 'I think it was a cold day, too, Joe. It was the middle of January last year, just before you were re-elected as Chair. Mind, when it came to the election to replace Les, I won't swear that she voted for you.'

'She can stick her vote. And I'm warning you

now, if she starts with me this weekend, I won't be responsible. I'll bury her.'

'Hark at Mr tough guy,' Brenda said. 'You'd be hard pressed to bury a bone for her dog.'

Before Joe could respond and to the disapproval of several customers, a bout of raucous laughter emanated from a corner table where Lee, taking an early break, sat with three male friends and a young woman.

Stood alongside Joe, keeping her voice down, Kayleigh scowled. 'Jess Collier. We know all about her on our estate. My Mam says she's a right van.'

Joe frowned. 'A van? You can get loads in her?'

Kayleigh was equally puzzled. 'No. You know what I mean, Uncle Joe. One of them thingies out of horror fillums. They eat the blood from your neck.'

'You mean a vampire,' he said. 'Or a vamp as such women are known.'

Kayleigh nodded. 'You don't have to worry. She don't go for old blokes, don't Jess.'

Joe grimaced at the reference to "old blokes".

Kayleigh was still speaking. 'You ask Cheryl about her, Uncle Joe. She was in the same class as Jess Collier at school.' She made her way to the kitchen and still keeping her voice down, said. 'Chezza. You know Jess Collier, don't you?'

Cheryl appeared and crossed to join Joe. With a scowl at the group in the far corner, she said, 'I know her all right. The way she carries on, she should be charging for it. She'd be a rich woman by now.'

35

'Who are the other three?' Joe asked.

'Three of Lee's rugby mates.'

As if on cue, another bout of deafening laughter came from the group.

His patience already hanging by a thread, Joe snapped to his feet and marched over to them. 'Keep the noise down, will you?'

'What's your problem, shorty?' demanded Jess Collier.

According to Joe's estimate, she would be twenty-eight years old, the same age as Lee and Cheryl. Her flaming red hair was cropped short, almost like boys'. A busty young woman showing far too leg under the hem of her miniskirt, her right arm was a mass of tattoos, amongst which was the club emblem of the Sanford Bulls.

'Call me that again, girl, and you'll find out how short I am when my boot connects with your backside.'

'You'll have to get through me first, pal,' said one of the other three, a tall, strapping young man with a head of close cropped fair hair.

Years of dealing with awkward, sometimes cantankerous customers meant that Joe would never back down. 'And who the hell do you think you are?' he snapped.

The youngster pointed a finger at his own chest. 'I'm Ian Grainger, pal. The toughest prop since this fella here.' He now pointed at Lee.

'Nark it, Grainger,' Lee warned. 'This is me Uncle Joe.'

'That's right. I own this place, and when you're here you do as I say not as you please.' Memory bells rang in Joe's head. 'And I thought you lot had a match in Bridlington.'

'They've time, Uncle Joe, and I'll make 'em behave,' Lee assured him before any of the others could answer. 'Let me tell you who they are.' He pointed at the young woman. 'This lass is Jess Collier, one of the Bulls' biggest fans.' Lee's finger tracked round the table. 'The one gobbing off at you is Ian Grainger, this'n is Niall "simple" Semple. He's our coach's lad.' Lee waved at the final member of the group. 'And this fella is Dave Drummond, Rott's younger brother. You remember Rott.'

In turn they nodded a mute greeting to Joe, who focussed on Drummond. 'I remember Rott all right. And you're his brother? Ollie's son-in-law?' When Drummond nodded, Joe went on. 'No matter who you are, you don't come in here upsetting my customers.'

'That's Uncle Joe's job,' Lee said, causing another chorus of laughter.

'And you can knock it off, too. What are you all doing here anyway? Shouldn't you be over at The Bullring?'

It was Semple who answered. 'The bus don't leave until eleven this morning. We just called to see if your Lee was coming with us.'

'I told 'em, Uncle Joe, I said you're going away with your old people's club, so I can't get there until tomorrow cos I have to run this place, and we'll be too late to catch the match.'

'And he won't be with them after the game,' Cheryl called from across the café. 'He'll be with

37

me, looking after Danny.'

'Correct,' Joe agreed. 'And they're not old people, they're 3rd agers.' He cast sour eyes around the group. 'They can drink young clowns like you lot under the table any time you choose. Now do as I say and keep the noise down.'

His face a mask of anger, he returned to his seat but he had no sooner sat down when Cheryl piped up. Pointing up at the wall clock she said, 'If you all don't get a move on, you won't see Angela Foster, the Sanford Bulls, or anyone else, cos the bus'll go without you.'

Joe checked the time and read 9:20. 'Hmm. Happen you're right.' He threw off his whites, hung them in the kitchen locker, took out his quilted topcoat and after checking his pockets to ensure he had everything he would need, said, 'When you're ready, ladies.'

The women followed his example, and a few minutes later, Joe bid the three remaining staff a final, 'See you in Bridlington tomorrow, Cheryl, and you after Easter, Kayleigh.'

Towing their small suitcases behind them, they stepped out into the chilly morning for the walk to the Miners Arms.

Chapter Four

With every excursion, no matter how long the duration, it fell to one of the three management members to check the passengers onto the coach as they arrived. In respect of the cloud promising a drop of rain, Joe allowed Sheila and Brenda to board the bus. Keith Lowry, the driver regularly appointed to Sanford 3rd Age Club outings, had the engine and heaters running, and the two women would be warmer, drier inside than out.

They were the first to arrive but while Joe and Keith stood smoking and chatting, others soon began to turn up, led by Alec and Julia Staines.

'You looking forward to Bridlington rather than Benidorm, then, Joe?' Alec asked as he left his two small suitcases and prepared to board. 'I hope you've brought your wallet with you cos Sheila and Brenda'll make you pay for trying to change the weekend and causing us all that grief in February.'

'What grief?'

Alec grinned. 'Well, it seemed to me that you weren't any too happy about it.'

'If I told you to get stuffed, Alec, would you be offended?'

'Not in the slightest, but I might decide to hike my prices ten percent the next time you're due to have The Lazy Luncheonette's kitchen walls repainted.'

The gag forced a smile from Keith. 'Is he incinerating you're a tightarse, Joe?'

'It's one of those scurrilous rumours that do the rounds, mate. I'm as generous as your average Ebenezer Scrooge.'

'One thing's for sure,' Keith grumbled, 'you've deffo got me working Monday, coming back to Bridlington to pick you up. I feel like, whoisit, Bob Scratch it.'

'Cratchit,' Joe corrected him. 'Bob Cratchit. And he was lucky. Old Scrooge gave him a day off… I think. I'd have had him working throughout. Anyway that was Christmas, not Easter.'

'This can't be Easter either. At least, it don't feel like it. It's more like the middle of rotten winter.'

From there a steady stream of members began to arrive and Joe focussed on checking their names on his list.

Another taxi pulled in and after paying the driver, Angela Foster climbed out, towing a small case behind her, which Keith took from her.

'Good morning, Mr Murray… Or should I call you Joe now that I'm a member of the 3rd Age Club?'

'No, no. You're fine with Mr Murray.' He ticked her name off his list, took a final drag on his cigarette, dropped it to the ground, and crushed the remains underfoot. Only then did he give her the least obsequious, most insincere smile he could muster.

While she wondered how to respond, Owen Frickley's Toyota pulled in and he and George Robson climbed out. Leaving Owen to lock the car up, George came to the bus, put his arm around

40

Angela's shoulder and joked, 'Joe driving you up the wall already, is he, Angie? Never mind, girl. You'll get used to him… in, say, about ten years.'

'I've already told Alec Staines where to get off,' Joe retorted, 'and you can join him.' He ticked off George and Owen, and ran an eye down his list. 'Only Tanner, Sylvia, Mad Mavis along with her bloke, Cyril Peck, and then Stewart Dalmer, and we're on our way, Keith.'

As he spoke more members arrived, and another taxi pulled in, dropping off Les Tanner and Sylvia Goodson.

It always seemed to Joe that the couple – one of Sanford's most open secrets – had a habit of dressing inappropriately for weekend outings. Most of the members would be clad in casual clothing. Joe, himself, wore a pair of jeans and a jumper, augmented by a fleece. That would not be fitting for former Captain Leslie Tanner (TAVR) or Sylvia Goodson.

Something of a hypochondriac (in Joe's narrow opinion) Sylvia was wrapped in a heavy, winter coat and a woolly bonnet. Tanner also sported a topcoat, but beneath it was his regimental blazer, a crisp, white shirt, and a navy blue tie. Beneath the hem of his overcoat, a pair of grey trousers were visible, the crease so sharp that Joe felt he would be able to shave with it, and at ground level, the captain's sensible, black shoes, gleamed with a mirror finish shine.

'Morning, Sylvia, morning, Les.'

Pulling two light suitcases, Tanner brushed past Joe with barely a nod of greeting, and joined

41

Keith at the luggage compartment.

'What's up with him?' Joe asked as Sylvia prepared to board the bus.

'I'm sorry, Joe. He's not well. Apparently he has a magnesium deficiency.'

Joe glanced back at Tanner. 'I thought he wasn't his usual bright spark self.'

He watched the pair climb on the bus, then spoke to Keith. 'Three more, buddy, and we're rolling.'

'Not a minute too soon, either,' Keith replied with a glance at his wristwatch.

Even as he spoke, two more taxis pulled in, one dropping off Mavis Barker and Cyril Peck, the second delivering the tall, imposing figure of local antiques dealer, Stewart Dalmer. Once they were aboard, Keith secured the luggage compartment, Joe climbed onto the bus, took the single seat across the narrow aisle from Sheila and Brenda, Keith settled behind the wheel, started the engine and to a muted cheer from the passengers, they pulled out of the car park and onto Doncaster Road towards Sanford town centre, from where they would pick up the York Road.

'What's up with Les?' Sheila asked. 'He never said a word when we spoke to him.'

'He did the same with me,' Joe admitted. 'According to Sylvia, he has a magnesium deficiency. Ex-part-time soldier, you'd think he'd have a flare gun somewhere, wouldn't you?'

Brenda frowned. 'Whatever for?'

'The flares are packed with magnesium. He could shove one—'

Sheila cut him off with a warning. 'Joe.'

He grinned at her. 'I was gonna say he could shove one in his pipe.'

Going via the route Keith had chosen, which would grant the passengers the time to grab a bite and a cup of tea and visit the toilet outside York, it was a journey of about eighty miles, and the driver assured Joe that on a Friday, and not just any Friday, but one of the country's major holiday weekends, it would take probably the better part of two and a half hours.

Heavy traffic through Sanford reminded Joe, but when he mentioned it, both women remained unmoved.

'The rest will do us good,' Brenda said. 'We have a lot of shopping to get through when we get there. Isn't that right, Sheila?'

'Absolutely. We'll keep you busy, Joe.'

'Native bearer?'

'Precisely,' Sheila agreed and both women laughed.

Joe did not mind. The last five weeks had seen Brenda come on in leaps and bounds. She had not entirely got over the nightmare of mid-February but with each passing day she was becoming more and more like her old self.

As the bus struggled through the town and then onto more open road, Brenda risked a glance over her shoulder, and content to see Angela Foster at the rear with George and Owen, she lowered her voice and asked, 'Did you play the proper gentleman with Angela, Joe?'

'Of course I did. We agreed that she can call

43

me Mr Murray, while I'll address her as You Judgemental Cow.'

Sheila did not find it funny. 'You'd better not.'

'I'm joking, woman. No matter how bad anyone treats me, I would never be that ignorant.'

Brenda shook her head. 'Yes you would. Bear in mind, Joe, we've known you for most of your life.'

'In that case, you must know about the good I do for the community.'

'Such as?'

'Well, I keep you two off the streets, for a start off.'

Sheila took instant umbrage. 'How dare you—'

Brenda interrupted. 'I don't think Joe's saying we'd be reduced to selling ourselves, dear. I think he means we'd both end up as bag ladies if he didn't keep us in work.'

Joe chuckled. 'I can just see you both dressed in cast offs, pushing a worn out supermarket trolley round Sanford, and doing a little dance while passersby drop pennies in your tatty carrier bag.'

It was left to Brenda to end the debate. 'Much more from you, Joe Murray, and you'll need help to push a new shopping trolley round Sanford.'

As their driver predicted, it would be a long and tedious journey taking a more northerly route via York, rather than the easterly route via Howden and Driffield. It allowed him a forty-five minute stop at a large café between York and Malton where his passengers could take in a snack and a cup of tea, and make use of the facilities.

It was during that stop that Joe received another text message.

Enjoy Brid. It might be your last.

When Brenda read it her features paled and he guessed she was thinking about her week of torturous incarceration.

Sheila was more practical. 'Cheryl told you, you should take it to the police, but you didn't bother did you? Instead, you argued back.'

'I was trying to bring him out into the open,' Joe argued.

'These people will never face you,' Brenda said. 'Oh, Joe, please call Gemma about it. If nothing else, it's a nuisance communication.'

Wishing he had not said anything about it, Joe capitulated. 'All right, all right. I'll have a word with her on Tuesday, when we're back in Sanford.'

It was a shade after one in the afternoon when Keith pulled in outside the International Hotel, overlooking Bridlington's North Beach.

As always, Joe was first off the coach, looking forward to speaking to Geoff Vallance's sister, but in this instance, not only was the woman not manning reception, but after the appraising the counter clerks of his identity, he insisted on hurrying to the toilets.

Consequently when Sheila ambled in after him, she was at a loss to spot him.

'He was in urgent need of the gents,' the young woman behind the reception desk told her.

'It's the only time you ever see Joe rushing anywhere. I'm Sheila Riley, part of the management trio for the Sanford 3rd Age Club. So

45

while were waiting for Joe, can we make a start on checking our members in? I've an idea there are about seventy of us.'

The receptionist was in the process of handing out registration cards when Joe returned. 'That was close,' he said, and Brenda, now stood alongside Sheila, could not help laughing.

'We keep him in nappies, you know,' she said to the reception clerk who blushed at the mental imagery Brenda's remark generated.

Ignoring Brenda, Joe asked, 'So where is Geoff's sister?'

'You mean Ms Vallance, sir? It's her lunch break. She'll be back on duty at two.'

As always the process took the better end of twenty minutes before Joe, always one of the last to be dealt with, finally walked into room 407. For once, he was pleased. On most outings, he ended up with a room overlooking the rear of the hotel, but this time he found himself with a pleasing view of the beach, Flamborough Head to his left, and the vast spread of the North Sea, the waves driven by a fresh breeze, while a weak, April sun tried to make a dent in the cloudy sky.

'You've travelled further and fared worse, Joe,' he said to the empty room.

He joined Sheila and Brenda in the hotel restaurant for a light lunch of cold cuts.

'The town centre's about half a mile down the road,' Sheila said at one point. 'What say we have a steady walk down there, grab a snack and see what the shops have to offer?'

'And at the risk of repeating myself, I suppose

you'll want me there to carry all your bags?' Joe asked.

'And pay for the snacks,' Brenda said with a chuckle. 'Why else would we need you? Anyway, if you do the honours, and carry the shopping around for us, Joe, I'll reward you for both of us.' With a saucy smile, she put a suggestive edge into her voice. 'You know you like it when I reward you.'

Joe laughed and Sheila frowned. 'You're incorrigible, the both of you,' she chastised them.

Brenda was more than equal to the challenge. 'And I've told you before, Sheila Riley, no one has ever tried to corrige me. Now are we going to make a move, or sit here all day wondering what the Easter bunny is going to bring us?'

'Make sure you wrap up warm,' Joe advised. 'It's not exactly freezing but there's a nippy wind blowing in off the sea and there's a drop of rain promised.'

'Not a problem,' Brenda declared. 'We can always duck in to Promenades, the local shopping mall.'

As they finished their meal, a woman entered the dining room. Clad in the Accomplus uniform, she was slender and according to Joe's estimate, about six feet tall. Fair-haired with a pleasant face, she looked around, and fixed her stare upon them.

She zigzagged through the various tables and stood alongside Sheila. 'Am I right in thinking it's Mr Murray, Mrs Riley, Mrs Jump?'

Joe studied her name tag. 'Spot on, Natalie. I have to say, you look almost as tall as your brother.'

'A matter of a few inches only, Mr Murray.'

'Please call me Joe.' He pointed between his two friends. 'It's preferable to some of the names they still call me.'

Brenda smiled at the moment. 'Take no notice, Natalie. Joe's spent years trying to get close to your sister-in-law, and always failed, so now he's going to pine for you.'

Raising her eyebrows for permission, she took the remaining seat at the table. 'Yvonne has always had that effect on older men.'

'Especially single old saddoes like him.' Brenda beamed a mock sweet smile on Joe.

Natalie was a good looking woman. Somewhere in her mid to late forties, slim, wide-eyed, a shower of pure blonde hair sweeping down over her shoulders, she was shapely and slender at the waist. The kind of woman who could turn men's heads... particularly Joe's.

Joe smiled upon her. 'You can ignore Brenda, Natalie,' he advised. 'She only gets jealous when there's a pretty woman like you around. How are Geoff and Yvonne?'

'Settled with each other, I'm pleased to say. Manning the battlements at the Palmer,' Natalie said. 'Not quite as busy as us, but it is Easter weekend so they'll be at it non-stop.'

And Brenda grinned again. 'So would Joe if he got the chance.'

Natalie ignored the innuendo. 'We've another busload due in any time now... Oh. You'll know anyway, won't you? It's that friend of yours. The one you mentioned on the phone the day you rang

48

me. Mr Ollister and his rugby team.'

It came as a slight surprise to all three, and Joe spoke first. 'The Sanford Bulls? We knew they were in town, but we didn't know they were staying here.'

'They have a match here tomorrow, so I'm told. Not,' Natalie went on, 'that it's any of our business. Ours is not to reason why but to pour more money into the Accomplus pie. Talking of which, I'd better get back to work.' She stood up. 'It's lovely to see you all. I've been looking forward to meeting you after listening to Yvonne's tales, and hey, you're in for some fabulous entertainment this weekend.'

Joe's smile broadened. 'You're gonna do some pole dancing for us?'

'Dream on,' Natalie replied with a laugh, and then left them.

'Smashing woman,' Joe approved when they were alone again.

'I don't know how these people tolerate your suggestive chatter,' Sheila complained.

'It's called fun, Sheila.'

'Until it goes too far.'

'Not much danger of that with a young woman like Natalie,' Brenda said. 'She'd have to be seriously hard up to take Joe on.'

He took the jibe with good humour. 'That's what I love about you, Brenda. The way you flatter me. Gives a real boost to my ego. Now come on. Drink up and let's get moving.'

Several minutes later, they were ready for leaving for the walk into Bridlington when Hayden Ollister appeared alongside their table.

'Now then, you three,' he greeted them. 'Glad to see you all here.'

'And we've just heard you were due in, but we'll have to catch up later. The girls need me to carry their shopping.'

Ollister's features darkened. 'Far be it from me to stand in your way, but is there any chance you can spare me a few minutes before you shoot off?'

Joe looked to the other two, who nodded. 'Give us a ring when you're ready,' Sheila suggested, 'and we'll let you know where to find us.'

Chapter Five

The women left, Joe and Ollister moved to the bar where the chairman of the Sanford Bulls signalled a waiter for drinks. Soon, supplied with beer, Joe got straight to the point.

'I don't have long. I want to catch up with the girls, so is there some problem, Ollie?'

'Aye, you might say that, Joe. First off, how's Brenda shaping up? She looked to me as if she's just about over that business in February.'

'Almost. She's getting there. Slow but sure. Anyway, never mind Brenda. There are plenty of folk looking out for her. What's wrong that you want to talk to me?'

Ollister did not answer. To Joe's irritated puzzlement, he left the table and approached the bar where it seemed he posed a question and listened to the answer. Satisfied, he returned to rejoin Joe.

'Just sorting summat out,' he explained as he took his seat again.

'You're also hedging,' Joe argued. 'What the hell's going on, Ollie?'

'Awkward this, Joe. I mean, I told you back in February about our Tilly and her husband, Dave.'

'You did. So what about them? Kissed and made up have they? Only Dave was in my place this morning. Him and a couple of other Bulls lads, and some young tart named Collier.'

'Jess Collier. I know her. We all do.' Ollister gave a sad shake of the head. 'And the other two were Ian Grainger and Niall Semple. I wondered where they'd got to. Anyway, we're talking about Tilly and Dave. Kissed and made up? It's exactly the opposite. They've split up.'

Wondering what he was supposed to say, Joe picked up his glass and took a large gulp. 'Sorry to hear that, mate. What pushed them over the edge?'

Ollister, still hesitant, also drank from his glass. 'My missus, Viv. Three nights back, about ten o'clock Tuesday, she saw Dave heading into the Rising Sun on West Street, and he had that little tramp with him. Collier. She's a raving Bulls fan. She follows us everywhere and she has a bit of a rep for being easy.'

'I've heard,' Joe commented.

Ollister let out a humourless chuckle. 'She's known as the Sanford Bulls' bike. Practically every lad on the team has had the pleasure if you know what I mean.'

Joe sneered. 'I think I can remember. Nowt much I can say, Ollie, except that Dave Drummond is a bloody fool and if your Tilly has thrown him, good on her. Was this Collier sort the one he was fooling around with before? The one you told me about in February?'

'According to Tilly, yes. Course, when our Viv saw them, she went and told Tilly, didn't she? There was a blazing row and Tilly told Dave to get out. She never wants to see him again. When I got to know, I tackled Dave and he says he don't know who the missus saw in Sanford, but it wasn't him. He was at The Bullring early in the evening, with your Lee, working out in the gym, and he says he

52

never went nowhere near Sanford town centre after that.' Ollister sighed. 'And this is the problem, Joe. I don't know. Dave's insistent that he's never had nowt to do with Collier, and he'll make life hell for Tilly if it comes to the divorce courts.'

Joe put on a deliberately thoughtful face. 'Tough one that. Any danger your missus could be mistaken?'

'It's possible but not likely. She's very protective of Tilly, is our Viv. Won't stand for anyone hurting the girl, and obviously, she knows Dave well. If she says it was him, then it was him... but I don't know. He's so damned determined that he's done nowt wrong. Anyway, Dave's shipped back to his mother's and the missus is staying with Tilly for now. Baby's due any time and we don't want her to be on her own.'

Joe did justice to the sympathy and then pointed to the bar. 'So what does this have to do with the hotel? I mean, why go nattering to the barman about it?'

'I wasn't. I was just asking if the bar is open to non-residents. It is.'

Joe's puzzlement grew. 'Yes? And?'

'Well, you know we've a match tomorrow, and I told you that this little tart, Collier follows us everywhere. She'll be in here tonight. Fact, I wouldn't be surprised to find she's here already, and I guarantee she'll turn up in this bar tonight because that's where me and the team will be.'

Joe's wrinkled brow creased further. 'Yes? And?'

Ollister put down his glass. 'Well, see, Joe, you

said you still work as a private eye. I thought while you're here, if you can show me that it was or wasn't Dave, settle it once and for all, one way or t'other, I can try and sort it out from there. You're here until Monday, aren't you, and I'm not asking you to give up your weekend for it, but if you could get me some answers, I'll pay you two ton. How's that sound?'

Joe shook his head sadly. 'I really must get myself a publicity agent. Everyone thinks I'm obsessed with money.'

'Well, you are, aren't you?'

'Bog off.' Joe took another wet of beer. 'You'll not hear me say this often but forget about money. I'll keep an eye out for this girl in the bar tonight and if she's there, if she's cosying up to Drummond, I'll give you the nod.'

'I don't need you to do that. I'll be in the bar myself. I'm thinking more if you spot him and her out and about in Bridlington. She's easy to recognise. One arm is covered in tattoos. From a distance, it looks like she's covered in pit muck and hasn't bothered to wash.'

Joe tutted. 'I told you, Ollie, I've met her. Gobby little cow she is, too.'

The rugby man shrugged. 'Fair enough. And as you might guess, she'll tell you where to go in as few words as possible.'

'Water off a duck's back, mate. The draymen do that every morning. Leave it to me.'

* * *

With the time pushing three o'clock, Joe ordered a

taxi to collect him at the International and take him to the Promenades shopping mall.

Hurrying through the hotel lobby, he was waylaid by the deputy general manager, Brian Lambert, a pleasant, easy going six footer, who aside from being pleased to see Joe and his 3rd Age Club members, proceeded to outline the weekend's events.

'A young lass named Rita Penney, Mr Murray. Smashing girl and she'll be putting out party music. What better way to get into the holiday spirit?'

Joe wasn't really listening. He nodded to give the impression that he was paying attention, but he was relieved when his taxi appeared. 'I'll catch you later, son,' he said and hurried out to the car.

Less than five minutes later, the cab dropped him outside the bus station and the rear entrance to Promenades, where he paid the driver and cursed himself for not realising how close the mall was to the International. He could have walked it in less than ten minutes.

Having phoned ahead, he knew exactly where to find the two women, but as he hurried into the shopping centre he found himself confronted with a crowd of people who seemed to be trying to calm a distressed woman, and in conjunction with the amount of onlookers, there was little space for others to pass by.

As he tried to force his way through, he heard a voice wailing, 'She's gone. My friend. She's been taken.'

Some people were muttering sympathetically, others less so, and Joe distinctly heard one man grumble, 'Another nutter on the loose. I don't know what this place is coming to.'

Joe knew otherwise. The moment the distraught woman cried out, he recognised her voice. Brenda.

He tried pushing his way into the crowd surrounding her, but was pushed back. Feeling his temper on the rise, he made another attempt, and one of the mall's security guards turned on him. 'Just clear off, pal, before I take the hump with you.'

'I know her, you idiot. She's a friend of mine. I can calm her down in a minute when you and these other morons get out of the way.'

'Now listen, pal—'

'Listening is what you want to try... *pal*. I just said, she's a friend of mine. I know what's wrong with her, and she needs to see someone she knows.'

Joe pushed his way into the crowd again, thrusting, shouldering people out of the way, ignoring their complaints, until he came face-to-face with Brenda.

Tears were streaming down her terrified face, sweat had broken out on her forehead, she was trembling, and according to Joe's way of thinking, on the verge of collapse. The security guard tried grabbing him. Joe shrugged him off, pushed a final brace of people out of the way, put his arms round her, and hugged her to him.

'Brenda. It's me. Joe. Come on now. Hold it together. I'm here. Nothing can hurt you.'

The grumbling, muttering around him increased, the security guard eyed him even more suspiciously, but then Brenda suddenly focused.

'Oh, Joe. Thank God you're here. Sheila's gone. She's been taken. That bitch is out, and she's taken Sheila.'

'Calm down. Just calm down. Take a couple of deep breaths. Sheila hasn't been taken. She's here somewhere. Deep breaths, Brenda. In through the nose, out through the mouth, slowly, in your own time, let it calm you down.' She began to obey, and Joe turned on the security guard. 'Any danger someone can get her a cup of tea.'

'Yes, but—'

'I know what's wrong with her, and it's nothing serious. Post-traumatic stress, if you really want to know. Now for crying out loud, someone get her a cup of tea.'

There was a bench nearby. Joe guided her to it, sat her down, crouched before her, and held her hands.

Brenda wept openly. 'She's gone, Joe. She was with me in Poundland, and then she was gone. That tart has taken her. I'm telling you.'

'No, Brenda. No one's taken her. She's probably still in the shop.'

An assistant from a nearby store arrived and passed a small cup of tea to Brenda. She held it in shaking hands, and sipped from the cup. 'No, Joe. How could she disappear like that? She's been kidnapped. Just like me.'

Joe kept his tones soft and soothing 'Calm down, Brenda. Come on now. Remember your breathing exercises. Drink your tea. It'll help you calm down and you'll see. She'll be back in a minute. Do your breathing exercise and drink that tea and be calm.'

Sniffing back her tears, the cup and saucer rattling in her trembling hands, Brenda took another wet of the tea, and Joe noticed that a number of people were still hanging round, amongst them the security guard.

'So, what's wrong with her?' the guard demanded. 'Penny short of a full pound, is she?'

With Brenda's anxiety in mind, Joe made a determined effort to control his anger. 'For your information, she was kidnapped two, three months ago, and she spent a week tied to a chair in an old army training base.' He registered the shock on the security man's face. 'You've never gone through anything like that, and neither have I, but I've seen what it's done to her, and me and her friends are the best ones to handle it. Now why don't you and all the rest of these clowns,' he waved at the small group still surrounding them, 'bugger off and leave us alone? She'll be all right in a few minutes.'

As the crowd began to slowly disperse, some of them grumbling at Joe's irascible attitude, so Sheila appeared, her face a mask of concern. When Brenda laid eyes upon her, she put down her cup of tea, got to her feet and rushed into Sheila's arms.

'I thought you'd gone. I thought she'd taken you. I was all alone.'

Sheila looked to Joe who shrugged. Keeping his voice low, he said, 'She was panicking when I got here. What happened to you? Where did you go?'

Sheila gestured with her eyes to the public toilets behind her. 'I had to go to the ladies. It was urgent and I did tell her, but she wasn't listening. You know what she's like when she's shopping.'

Joe nodded. 'She's not as far forward as we thought. I think we still need to keep an eye on her, and it'll be like that for the foreseeable future.' He looked further along the mall. 'There's a café along there. Let's get her sat at a table, get her another cup of tea, and maybe a biscuit or something.'

He returned the cup and saucer to the shop assistant, thanked her, and with Sheila's help, got Brenda to her feet, and under the interested eyes of many people, walked with their shaky, distressed friend along the mall to the cafeteria.

Even with hot drinks and snacks, it took a good twenty minutes for Brenda to fully calm down, and during which period, she was full of embarrassed apologies.

'I made a total fool of myself, haven't I?' she said when she was back to something like her usual self.

'You're not well, dear,' Sheila told her. 'And since when did we ever worry about other people's opinions?'

Joe agreed with an encouraging smile. 'It's not the first time you've made a fool of yourself, Brenda, but at least this time it's not booze.'

A thin smile spread across her lips, and both Sheila and Joe took it as a sign of encouragement. 'Where would I be without you two?'

'Well,' Joe ventured, 'if it was left to that security bod, you'd be on your way to the nuthouse. Now, come on, girl. You're with us. No harm will come to you while we're here.'

59

Brenda leaned across, pecked him on the cheek. 'I love you, Joe Murray. Talking of which, where were you when Sheila did a runner? If you'd been with me, I wouldn't have got into that state.'

'That's right. Blame me. What else am I good for?' Pleased to see her coming back to her usual self, Joe grinned to show he was only joking. 'It was Ollie's fault. It seems Dave Drummond and Tilly have split up.'

'Well, what use does he think you can be?' Brenda said.

'He wants me to prove Dave Drummond is guilty or innocent as the case may be. Anyway, never mind him. We're more concerned about you.' Unwilling to get into the debate for the moment, he made his way into the café, ordered fresh coffee for himself and the two women, a second selection of biscuits, and rejoined them a few minutes later.

'So come on, Joe,' Sheila invited. 'Give us all the dirt on Ollie's son-in-law. Dave Drummond, you said? Rott's brother, isn't he?'

'The same,' Joe agreed as he broke open a small packet of oatmeal biscuits, helped himself, and pushed the other two into the middle of the table. 'It seems, Ollie's wife saw Dave out with this Jess Collier woman – her as was making all the noise in The Lazy Luncheonette this morning – and that was it. Drummond out the door.'

Sheila clucked. 'I know Vivienne Ollister. A proper matriarch, and she wouldn't hesitate to tell her daughter what she'd seen.'

'You're right. She didn't. Anyway, Ollie thinks she might be wrong, so he's asked me to keep my eyes open. If I'm right and Viv's wrong, I'm on two hundred dabs.' He grinned at Brenda.

'Don't count your chickens, Joe,' Brenda advised. 'Or your pound notes. I know Viv, too, and it's not often she's wrong.'

'It's not often I'm wrong, either, but it has been known.'

Joe's comment brought chuckles from both women.

As they finished their drinks, the two women made their way to the toilets, returned a few minutes later, and Brenda checked her watch.

'We'd better get moving,' she announced. 'It'll be dark soon.'

Another sign of her anxiety was how Joe read the comment. 'It's April and it doesn't get dark until turned eight o'clock. Having said that, it's turned four, so if you two are all shopped out, what say we have a steady stroll back to the hotel?'

The women agreed and began to gather together their belongings.

'What's the entertainment at the hotel tonight, Joe?' Sheila asked.

Joe racked his memory. 'I, er, some woman singer promising numbers from the Easter musicals... I think' Joe shrugged. 'I didn't know there were any Easter musicals.'

'Scrooged springs to mind,' Brenda said. A sarky grin came to her lips. 'Course, Scrooge was an amateur in your book, wasn't he, Joe?'

Sheila joined in the good-natured ribbing. 'If they based it on Joe's penny-pinching ability, it would have been a horror story.'

'Scrooge was Christmas, not Easter, and trust me, one day, you'll see that I've got it right.' Joe zipped up his quilted coat. 'Are we ready?'

Fifteen minutes later, they turned into the hotel car park, and as they did, they spotted two people apparently fighting.

'In broad bloody daylight,' Joe grumbled.

There was no one else inside, they were along the side of the hotel, out of sight of the entrance. Tussling with each other, one, the taller, slimmer of the pair, was trying to steal the other's handbag.

'Isn't that Angela Foster?' Sheila asked.

Joe studied the pair. 'Nah. No way is Angie that thin, or that tall.'

'I meant the other one, you idiot. That one that's…' Realisation dawned on all three at once, but it was Sheila who announced it. 'Oh, my God. It's a mugging.'

They began to run, and Joe shouted. 'Hey, you two. Knock it off.'

Unfortunately, his warning proved to be the distraction the thief needed. Angela looked their way, her opponent snatched one last time at the handbag, landed out a punch, and as Angela reeled and sank to the ground, the mugger ran off towards the promenade.

Joe handed over the bags he was carrying, and went off in pursuit. While the two women, hurried to assist Angela.

'Are you all right?' Brenda asked as they helped the distraught woman to her feet.

She was in a flood of tears. 'He's taken off with everything I had with me. Purse, cards, the lot.'

'Are you hurt?' Sheila asked.

Angela rubbed at her cheek where a bruise had begun to appear. 'It's nothing. I'm more concerned about everything else. My phone is in the bag. The rotten sod's got away with everything. I can't even stop my cards.'

'We've got phones, Angela,' Sheila said. 'Let's get you inside, and then we can call the police, and you can use my phone to ring your bank and credit card lines.'

Angela began to cry again. 'I don't have the numbers.'

'Stop worrying,' Brenda said. 'We can speak to Natalie, the general manager here. She'll dig them out for you. Now come on.'

At that point, a breathless Joe returned shaking his head. 'Too fast for me,' he said, and focused on Angela. 'Are you all right, luv?'

She drew in a shuddering breath. 'I'll be all right, thank you, Mr Murray.'

'Let's forget the Mr Murray business, huh? It's Joe.'

'Angela has quite a bit of ringing around to deal with, Joe,' Sheila said. 'Let's get inside, and if you could arrange sweet tea for her, we'll get on with calling the police and what have you.'

'Yeah. No problem. Let's move.'

Chapter Six

While the two women assisted Angela, Joe collected all the carrier bags and followed them into the hotel lobby where he left them at a table, and approached Brian Lambert on reception. Once he'd explained the situation, Brian rang through to the bar to arrange hot, sweet drinks for them, and then rang the police on their behalf.

'The drinks will be with you soon, Mr Murray, and the police are sending a couple of officers out to speak to Mrs Foster.'

'Thanks, fella. The usual, top drawer service from Accomplus, especially when friends of Geoff and Yvonne Vallance are in charge.' Joe was reminded of something which had occurred to him while he was chasing the mugger. 'Do you have CCTV covering the side of the building?'

Brian shook his head. 'Not specifically, but we do have cameras on the car park, and there's always the chance that one of those caught the incident. I'll speak to Natalie, and we'll get a look at them. If anything shows up, we'll copy it for the police.'

'Good on you.'

Joe returned to his friends and the distressed Angela, and gave them a rundown on Brian's actions, and concluded, 'Marvellous ruddy weekend this is turning out to be innit? Brenda throwing a wobbler, Angela mugged. I told you we should have gone to Benidorm.'

'Oh do shut up, Joe,' Brenda growled. 'This

poor woman's just been mugged.'

It was significant that her anxiety of an hour previously was gone. Her natural concern for others, a facet of her character she shared with Sheila, was overriding earlier events, and although he did not say so, Joe was pleased to see it.

He focussed on Angela. 'I can't say we'll get your belongings back, but with a bit of luck, the local filth might have an angle, especially if the car park CCTV turns up anything.'

Angela nodded her thanks. 'I don't know what I'm gonna do in the meantime. I don't even have a debit card I can use in the hotel's ATM.'

'Stop worrying about that,' Joe reassured her. 'We'll have a word with our members and organise a whip round for you.'

The tears began to flow again as a waiter delivered hot drinks for them. 'I never realised just how supportive of each other you people are.'

Brenda poured out a cup of tea for her. 'Get some sugar in that, Angela. It's good for a shock, so we're told. And as for the club, a lot of people in Sanford see us as a mob of born again teenagers, but that's a long way from the truth. Sure, we like a good time, and fair few of our people like to sink as much ale as they can, but when things go astray, we close ranks. Isn't that right, Joe, Sheila?'

He chuckled. 'By and large, yes. Course, when you're busy investigating the murder of a musician, and the club thinks you should be chasing after Mort Norris because they suspect he has a bit on the side, the sparks can fly.'

Both Sheila and Brenda laughed. 'That

happened in Cleethorpes,' Sheila explained. 'To be fair, however, Joe did solve both problems, didn't you, dear?'

Listening to the tale, Angela focused on Joe. 'I must say, you weren't slow to chase after the attacker. Quite surprising considering how much you don't like me.'

With a grim smile, he grunted. 'Let's just say that's all water under the bridge, Angela.'

Angela returned the smile. 'Well, the next time you want to join my dating agency, I'll do you a special offer.'

Brenda could not help laughing. 'He doesn't need dating agencies, love. He's got a string of concubines from Sanford to Scarborough and back, and at least one lover in Tenerife.'

'You're getting me a reputation I can do without,' Joe retorted.

Several minutes later, Natalie arrived and sat with them. After apologising to Angela, she said, 'We have the incident on CCTV, but it's quite some distance from the hotel. It's the camera close to the road.' She held up a memory stick. 'I've copied it onto this and when the police arrive I'll hand it over to them. Again, Mrs Foster—'

'It's Ms Foster, Ms Vallance. I'm not married. Well, not these days.'

'Fine. But I was saying, I have to apologise again on behalf of the Accomplus group, and this hotel in particular. We take the security of our guests quite seriously, and if we can help in any way, please, don't hesitate to ask.'

'Is there is one thing you could do, Natalie,' Joe

said. 'Angela has lost everything. Money, credit cards, her phone, the lot. Could you provide her with funds, on the basis of contacting her bank first thing in the morning and having them transfer the money back to you?'

Natalie checked her watch. 'It's not yet five o'clock. Is there any chance they'll be there now, Ms Foster?'

'They might be, but I don't have any of the references. Account numbers and so on. I don't even have their phone number.'

Joe intervened again. 'There are ways and means of getting round that,' he told her as he got to his feet. 'Come on. Let's go to Natalie's secret lair, and phone your bank.'

Left at the table, Sheila and Brenda watched the trio disappear behind reception and into Natalie's private office.

'You think Joe's getting sweet on her?' Sheila asked. 'Angela, I mean, not Natalie.'

Brenda laughed out loud. 'You never know with that man.' She mock-tutted. 'And after this afternoon, I was hoping to have him all to myself for the rest of the weekend.'

'Again?'

'Sheila, he's been a rock since...' Brenda trailed off as the memories struck home. 'Since what happened. Hell you saw him in the shopping mall earlier. When I couldn't find you, I was a panic stricken wreck, but Joe...' A wistful smile crossed her lips. 'Despite his grumpiness, he'd make some woman a good husband.'

'But not you?'

67

'Dear me, no. I'm just happy to thank him now and then.'

Sheila frowned. 'More now than then these days.'

A quarter of an hour later, as the police arrived, Joe and Angela rejoined the two women.

'They sorted me out,' Angela said. 'A couple of hundred pounds, but it'll see me for the weekend.' She smiled on Joe. 'Thank you, Joe. I don't think I could have got through that without you.'

'That's what I'm here for. Getting other people out of the mire,' he told her as the police left the reception counter and made their way across the lobby to join them. 'And the minute these guys are done with us, I'm away to my room to catch up on a bit of kip.'

Twenty minutes later, having told the police all he knew, he returned to his room, stripped down to his underwear, climbed beneath the duvet and let sleep wash over him.

A call from Sheila woke him at just after six. She told him she'd arranged for Angela to join them for dinner, and after grumbling about it, Joe cut the call, took a shower, shaved and dressed for the evening in a pair of black pants and a thick jumper, topped up by his ever-present gilet, its pockets crammed with the usual accoutrements of cigarette papers, disposable lighters, tobacco, and a salbutamol inhaler to combat the effects of tobacco on his tortured lungs.

'Still smoking? You're a rotten idiot,' he cursed himself as he made his way to the ground floor lobby.

The evening meal was up to the usual Accomplus standard, while the three women opted for a variety of courses, Joe, in passing complement to the seaside location, chose deep-fried cod in batter, with chips, and a small selection of vegetables.

During the meal, the three women kept up a lively conversation on the pleasure of being away from Sanford by way of a change. There were frequent interruptions from other members, all of them asking after Angela's well-being, and commiserating upon the attack.

Joe was distracted by an interruption from Hayden Ollister, who crouched on his haunches alongside Joe, keeping his voice down, said, 'If you check the table closest to the exit, you'll see Jess collier with Dave Drummond, Willie Wilde, and Niall Semple.'

Joe clucked. 'Thanks, Ollie. I'll try and get a natter with them when I've finished my dinner.'

Once the meal was over, leaving the women to finish their wine, he excused himself, saying, 'Just nipping out for a smoke.' It was an adequate excuse, which would give him the opportunity to speak to Jess Collier and Dave Drummond, but as he left the table, he noticed that both she and the three Bulls' players she was sat with, had all gone.

He nevertheless took himself out to the smoke shelter where he found Les Tanner puffing contentedly on his pipe, and Alec Staines enjoying a cigarette. Lighting one of his hand-rolled smokes, Joe joined them.

'Tell you what, Joe,' Alec said, 'I don't know where that wind is coming from, but I know where it's going.'

Joe let out a stream of smoke. 'It's coming straight from Norway. I ordered it. Serves you lot right for not letting me go to Benidorm.'

Tanner looked down upon Joe. 'Oh, come on, Murray. What does Benidorm have that Bridlington doesn't?'

'You've got time to waste while I list everything?'

There was a long history of supposed animosity between Joe and the former TAVR captain, but it was mostly superficial. Tanner, head of the payroll department at Sanford Borough Council, disliked Joe's lack of administrative organisation, and Joe considered the captain to be symptomatic of the town hall's pen pushing, nitpicking crew. If push came to shove, both would defend the other.

Joe diverted Tanner's attention. 'Sylvia tells me you have minor health problems, Les.'

'Magnesium deficiency. Not serious, but it needs attention. I'm swallowing this disgusting supplement which I have to take twice a day. Worse than the tea in that café of yours. And before you get on about my military career, I've already heard all the magnesium flare jokes.'

Joe maintained an air of innocence. 'I was going to suggest where you could stick one.'

In the light of Tanner's scowl, it was Alec who changed the subject this time, heading off any potential argument. 'Sheila was talking to Julia earlier, and she told her that Brenda had a bit of a

70

turn in the shopping centre.'

Joe's features darkened. 'She's not over the other business yet, Alec. Not properly. When I got there, she was having a panic attack.'

'But she's all right now?' Tanner asked.

'Me and Sheila helped calm her down, thanks, Les.'

Alec spoke up again. 'And on top of that, Angie Foster got mugged? She must be shaken up by that.'

'I think she's all right, mate. Sheila and Brenda are looking after her.' Joe chuckled. 'And with Brenda back on form, that means Angie will be well tanked up by closing time.' He changed the subject again. 'Tell you what, I wanted a word with that young lass who was sat with Dave Drummond and a couple of the other rugby lads, but they've gone. All of 'em. You haven't seen anything of her, have you?'

Tanner frowned, Alec laughed. 'I haven't even looked,' Alec said. 'Fancy your chances, do you, Joe?'

'Don't talk bloody daft. It's something Ollie said to me earlier today. And before you ask, no, I can't say any more than that.'

The other two exchanged knowing glances. 'He's playing private eye again,' Tanner said.

'Not really,' Joe said. 'Playing at work is your forte, Les, not mine. When I take a job on, I do the job.' He crushed out the remains of his cigarette. 'Time I was getting back inside where it's warm. I'll catch you both in the bar later.'

Once back inside, he discovered that Sheila and Brenda had already made their way to the bar, but there was no sign of Angela. He joined them, signalled a waiter, and ordered drinks for the table, and then looked around.

Earlier in the day the tables at been evenly spread around the vast room. Now, they had been contracted towards the rear sides, leaving a space in front of the low stage. A dancefloor, Joe guessed.

'So where's Angela?' he asked as the drinks were delivered.

'She had to go back to her room,' Sheila replied, and with a glance at her watch, pursed her lips. 'She never said why, but she's been gone quite some time now. Hasn't she, Brenda?'

'The better end of an hour, I reckon,' her best friend agreed. 'Missing her, Joe? Maybe you thought it was your lucky night? Not two but three delightful dollies you could boogie the night away with.'

He pretend yawned. 'Two, three, bring another four if you like. I can cope.'

Angela returned at a couple of minutes after eight. She appeared flushed and flustered, and Joe automatically assumed it was the stress of the attack upon her earlier in the day. Barely had she settled down with a glass of white wine than the evening's entertainment got under way.

Joe recalled that at the Palmer they employed a resident DJ, but here it was left to Brian Lambert to take the stage and introduce Rita Penney, a twenty-something singer. The moment she appeared, Joe felt his interest evaporate. A young woman like that would not put out the kind of music he preferred.

The woman herself confirmed as much when

she shouted into the mic, 'Hit the floor people, and let's get this party moving with Whitney Houton and *I Wanna Dance With Somebody.*'

As the music began to pour from her backing track, younger people, a number of them from the Sanford Bulls took to the dance floor.

Brenda, her face flushed with immediate enthusiasm, turned on Joe. 'I thought you said Easter musicals?'

'That's what that Lambert guy told me... I think. Tell the truth, I wasn't really listening. I was more concerned with catching up with you two.'

Brenda smacked her lips. 'Who cares? This is my kinda stuff.' She got to her feet. 'Come on, Sheila. Let's show 'em how it's done.'

The two women left the table, and could be seen jiggling around the floor with George Robson and Owen Frickley.

'Not your kind of music, Joe?' Angela asked.

He shook his head. 'I'm more your Abba, Neil diamond, Freddie Mercury type of thing. You?'

'I don't mind this kind of music, but I'm too old for dancing around the floor like your two friends.' She took a sip of wine. 'I never thanked you properly for chasing after that idiot earlier.'

Given their past history, Joe felt uncomfortable left alone with her. As always in such situations, he retreated into the safe area of the 3rd Age Club. 'We're like that, us Sanford 3rd Agers. You pick on one member of the club and you pick on them all.'

There was silence for a minute or two while they watched the antics on the dancefloor.

Angela broke it. 'Look, Joe, about that time

73

when you applied to join my agency—'

He cut in before she could go on. 'I said before, it's water under the bridge, so let's forget about it, eh?' He chuckled. 'I'm no handsome hunk, and at the time, I was under an awful lot of stress. That idiot, Roy Vickers, had accused me of murder, the berk.'

'You did get it sorted, though, didn't you?'

Joe could not help a flush of pride showing through his words. 'Not only did I prove myself innocent, but I led Vickers to the real killer. It's what I do.' He took a sip of beer and leaned his elbows on the table. 'It's why I chased after that idiot earlier today. I believe in justice, and I can't stand by and watch other people attacked, hurt, robbed, whatever. And trust me, I'm not much use in a fight, but I've never lacked bottle.'

The music changed to *Toxic* by Britney Spears, but no one seemed inclined to leave the dancefloor. At the table, Joe changed the subject. 'So, how's business?'

'Not too bad. Like a lot of other industries, dating agencies tend to have the odd slack periods. And, as I'm sure I'd told you, I do secretarial and proofing work for a number of people. That's fairly quiet, too. I make a living, Joe, I don't think it's anywhere near your level of income.'

Now he laughed. 'Don't believe what other people tell you. The Lazy Luncheonette is a goldmine but it hasn't made me a millionaire yet.'

Sheila and Brenda returned from the dancefloor, both of them elated, smiling, and out of breath.

'Has Joe been sweet talking you, Angela?' Brenda asked.

'We've been having a bit of a chat, yes.'

Brenda grinned. 'Well, make sure your knickers are welded into place because when Joe turns the charm on, no woman can resist him.'

Joe returned the grin. 'And Brenda should know. She's never been able to resist me.'

The evening continued in the same vein, with Ms Penney putting out songs by the likes of Billie Eilish, Kylie Minogue, Diana Ross. Joe sat it out with Angela, Sheila had also had enough of dancefloor exercise, but Brenda took to the floor another couple of times, once with George Robson, and again with one of the younger men from Sanford Bulls.

'Eddie Allrodd,' she explained when she returned to the table. 'I used to go out with his father, years ago. Before I ever met Colin.'

'Proper little trip down memory lane, then,' Sheila observed.

A mysterious glint came to Brenda's eyes. 'I can safely say that I taught Vic Allrodd everything a man needs to know about keeping a young lady happy.'

'And he had the right surname for you, didn't he, Brenda?' Joe quipped.

She put on a look of innocence. 'As I recall, his name was an overstatement.'

The deliberate innuendo brought a round of laughter from the table.

As the minute hand on the hotel clock registered the half-hour, the drink and humour flowing freely round the room, Natalie appeared with two others, a man and a woman, in tow.

Natalie gestured at Angela. 'This is Ms Foster, Inspector.'

Joe's senses came to full alert at the mention of the woman's title.

Tall, slender, a mop of black hair, tied at the back of her neck, she was dressed against the cold, her hands thrust deep in the pockets of a quilted overcoat.

She withdrew her right hand, and showed her warrant card. 'I'm Detective Inspector Freya Elliman, North Yorkshire Police, and this is Detective Sergeant Buttle. I'll have to ask you to come with us, Ms Foster.'

Puzzled, alarmed, Angela began to rise from her seat, but Joe stepped in right away. 'Why do you want to speak to her?'

The inspector glared. 'Is that any of your business?'

'I'm making it my business. Angela is a friend, and trust me, I know about the law. You want to speak to her, fine, but she is entitled to know why.'

Freya sighed, and when she spoke again, it was directly to Angela. 'I need to question you on the murder of Jessica Collier.'

Chapter Seven

Joe noticed that moments before Freya made her devastating announcement, Natalie hurried round the room to the stage, and as Rita Penney ended her impression of Diana Ross, Natalie whispered in her ear. It made sense to Joe. The hotel manager already knew why the police were there, and she guessed that Freya's challenge would create a furore.

It was predictable. The moment Freya mentioned the words "murder of Jessica Collier" there was an immediate uproar at the table which drew the attention of other, nearer guests.

Angela raised her voice above the clamour. 'What are you talking about? I've never heard of Jessica Collier.'

'We believe differently, Ms Foster, and we urgently need to speak to you, now. If you refuse, I'll arrest you on suspicion and take you down to the station.'

Sheila and Brenda were making their vocal presence felt, Julia Staines and Les Tanner came to the table to join the discussion, and Joe raised his voice above them all, drowning out the singing of Rita Penney.

'Just shut up a minute, all of you,' he ordered, and then faced the inspector. 'What makes you think that Angela is involved in this girl's death?'

'Once again, Mr…'

'Murray. Joe Murray. That name might not mean anything to you, Inspector, but if you ring the police in Sanford, asked to speak to Detective Inspector Craddock, she'll vouch for me. When it comes to crime, I know what I'm talking about.' He swung his attention upon Angela. 'You have no choice, Angela, but to speak to them. However you are entitled to have someone with you. Do yourself a favour. Don't go to the expense of a lawyer. Pick me as your representative. I'll tie these people in so many knots, it'll take them until midsummer to untangle them.' He focused on the police again. 'I assume Natalie Vallance has allocated you somewhere where you can speak to Angela?'

Freya's features soured. 'You sound like exactly the kind of smartarse who'll make my life hell.'

'I repeat, speak to Inspector Craddock in Sanford. Yes, I'll make your life hell, but in the long run you'll find I'm more of an asset than a liability.' He got to his feet and gestured for Angela to join him. 'Lead on,' he said to Freya.

With police either side of them, they were led from the bar to reception, where Brian Lambert lifted the counter flap and gestured towards the rear room. 'It's my office, Inspector. A bit cramped, but you should manage.' His eyes fell on Joe. 'Oh, no. Don't tell me this is a repeat of that business at the Palmer that Yvonne and Geoff Vallance are always telling us about.'

Joe smiled. 'Not quite, Brian, but the filth—' his pointing finger wagged between the two police officers, '— have got it wrong… Again.'

There was no mistaking the venom in Tom Buttle's voice. 'Cocky little snot, aren't you?'

78

Joe agreed. 'True, but you'll learn I'm more often right than wrong, and if you don't believe me, forget DI Craddock, and try talking to the station commander in Sanford. Chief Superintendent Terry Cummins. He's known me since he was beat bobby.'

Lambert was right when he said the office was small and cramped. The obligatory box files lined shelves on three of the four walls, and the only window was small, inlaid with frosted glass. There were only three seats available, but Lambert, ahead of the game, brought in a fourth, which Joe dragged to the opposite side of the desk next to Angela. As always, the police sat between them and the exit.

Opening her pocketbook, Freya led the session. 'At about 8:45 this evening, the body of Jessica Collier was found on the beach about a hundred yards from here. Amongst her possessions we found a handbag, which, when we checked it, turned out to be your property, Ms Foster. If you're wondering how we knew the dead woman's identity, we found her driver's licence amongst her personal effects. To backtrack a little, at about four thirty this afternoon we had a report of a mugging, a robbery here at the International. That report came from you, Ms Foster. You gave a statement to one of our uniformed colleagues, backed up by statements from your friend here—' she gestured at Joe as she checked her pocketbook again '—and two other persons, Mrs Brenda Jump and Mrs Sheila Riley.' While she closed her pocketbook, Buttle opened his and made ready with his pen, and Freya went on, 'In your statement you claimed that you did not recognise your attacker. I think you did, Ms Foster. I think you recognised her as Jessica Collier, who – as it happens – was also from Sanford and was here with the Sanford Bulls, your rugby team. I think you not only recognised her, but when she left the hotel after dinner, you followed her and strangled her.'

'I did not. I told you, I don't even know the woman.'

'And I don't believe you.'

At this point, Joe interrupted proceedings. 'Just a minute. You're saying that this Collier woman mugged Angela, and when Angela caught up with her she still had the stolen handbag on her?'

'Mr Murray, you're here as a representative of Ms Foster. You're not a lawyer, and you can't interrupt—'

'Yes I can, especially if you're talking out of your backside. She went out, strangled Jessica, and then legged it without taking her handbag back? You're crediting Angela with the intelligence of a gormless idiot, and I know for a fact that she isn't one.'

'For all we know, she might have been interrupted by witnesses,' Buttle pointed out.

'And you have statements from these witnesses?' Joe demanded. 'Like I said, you're talking rubbish. Anyway, Angela was with me, Mrs Jump, and Mrs Riley at the time.'

Angela shook her head. 'Not all the time, Joe. I had to go back to my room, if you remember, but that's the only place I went.'

Freya's features, focused on Joe, betrayed a massive sense of superiority. 'Any further

80

objections, Mr Murray?'

'Yep, but I'll let you reel out enough rope to hang yourselves with.' He looked to Angela. 'Why did you go back to your room?'

She hesitated. 'I'd rather not say.'

Freya took the lead once more. 'In that case, Ms Foster, you're leaving yourself wide open to a possible charge of murder.'

Angela's anxiety began to show through. 'It wasn't me. I told you, I had to go back to my room, and that is the only place I went. But for God's sake, if I left the hotel, you'll find me doing so on their CCTV.'

Joe made an effort to encourage her. 'Listen, Angela, I don't know why you went back to your room. It's obviously something personal, but if you don't tell them, they'll keep running away with this idiotic idea that you topped the girl. Don't worry about me. I won't say anything to anyone. Just tell them why you went back to your room.'

The muscles of her face began to work agitatedly, her eyes darted around the room, and a blush came to her cheeks. 'I'd rather not say.'

To Joe's surprise, it was Buttle who encouraged her. 'If you don't tell us, love, you'll leave us to draw our own conclusions.'

Angela remained silent yet again, until the pressure ball eyes upon her began to tell, and when she finally spoke, it was with furious embarrassment. 'I have an unfortunate infection. It's common in older people like me. I had dinner with Mr Murray, Mrs Jump, Mrs Riley, and I had to go back to my room to change my underwear.'

Freya snorted. 'You're telling us that you wet yourself?'

Joe chimed in again. 'Don't knock it unless you've been there. I've just come through the better part of a year with similar problems and I'm still wearing incontinence pants. It's no laughing matter, and it's no subject for that kind of sneering from you.' He leaned forward, aimed an accusing finger at the police officers. 'I've been where she is, and it's not pleasant, but one thing I will guarantee. If you check her clothing, you'll find the relevant underwear either tucked away in a waterproof bag for carrying home, or hanging on one of the radiators having been washed through. What's more, if you speak to Natalie Vallance, or Brian Lambert get them to access the CCTV footage from all over this hotel, you'll find that she never left the building.'

'Mr Murray—' Freya began, only to be cut off by Joe.

'I can tell you a lot more, too. How much do you know about Jess Collier? Bugger all, I'll bet. Well, I know quite a bit about her. She's gobby, and has a reputation as a tramp, and you're wrong about her coming here with the Sanford Bulls. She's a fanatic about them, yes, but she doesn't travel with them. She just follows them everywhere, and according to legend, she's slept with more than one of the team. What price she was twisting one of the players' arms for something more than the odd bit of horizontal? Have you questioned any of them yet? No. Have you hell as like. Because like all cops, you've picked up on one strand, and gone to town on it.'

Buttle made an effort at mediation. 'No one's accusing Ms Foster of anything, Mr Murray.'

'Yes you are,' Joe argued, pointing an accusing finger at Freya. 'At least twice, your boss has said she doesn't believe Angela and she actually accused her outright.'

'Enough.' Freya slapped her hand on the desk to reinforce her decision. 'If you're so knowledgeable, Mr Murray, you'll understand the term, "person of interest".'

Joe effected a yawn. 'Been there. More times than you've issued parking tickets. Yes, and both times, I managed to make the police look the bloody fools that they were. You're saying Angela is a person of interest?'

'She is.' Freya swung her attention back to Angela. 'I need a full statement from you of your whereabouts between, let's say half past six and half past eight this evening. After that, we'll take our leave of you, but you must stay in the Bridlington area for the time being, and if you do go back to Sanford, we'll need to know about it so we can inform the local police.'

Angela bristled. 'This is absurd.'

Joe made another effort to calm her. 'Listen to the voice of experience, love. Give them their statement, and we can get on with our weekend, but you have my assurance that it won't end here.' He laid defiant eyes on the police. 'If they're not prepared to look anywhere else, I am, and I guarantee I'll clear your name.'

* * *

In the bar, Brenda looked anxiously at her watch. 'What's taking them so long?'

For the majority, interest in Rita Penney had faded, and only a few younger people were still moving around the dancefloor. Since Joe and Angela's departure, Les Tanner and his partner, Sylvia Goodson had joined Sheila and Brenda, and none of them were willing to believe that Angela Foster could have committed such a crime.

Sheila was more practical. 'You know the procedure, Brenda. I imagine that Angela is a person of interest. I don't doubt that she is innocent, but if the police have any evidence linking her to the dead woman, then they're duty-bound to question her.'

'She does have Murray with her,' Tanner pointed out. 'As you know, he and I don't always see eye to eye, but when it comes to this kind of problem, I have to admit that he's in a class of his own. They won't get away with any arm-twisting while he's there.'

'Do we know anything about this dead woman, this Jessica Collier?' Sylvia asked.

Brenda shook her head. 'Never heard of her.'

In response to her best friend's suspicion, Sheila frowned her disapproval. 'Of course you've heard of her. She was in The Lazy Luncheonette this morning with those friends of Lee's. Joe had to tell them to be quiet and she gave him short shrift. She's some kind of Bulls fanatic.'

Realisation dawned in Brenda's eyes. 'Oh.

Yes. Right. She's the one suspected of wrecking Dave Drummond's marriage. A lady with busy knickers according to what Cheryl and Kayleigh told us.'

It was Sylvia's turn to disapprove. 'Really, Brenda, that's a terrible thing to say about the poor woman.'

Sheila came down on her friend's side this time. 'Unfortunately, Sylvia, it's exactly the way she was described to us. Beyond that, we don't know anything about her, but if it's true, then I think her attacker is more likely to be one of the rugby players than Angela.'

Les Tanner made a show of filling his pipe bowl. 'Time I was stepping outside for a contemplative smoke, but I think that conclusion is unlikely, my dear. Yes, rugby is a tough game, but it is only a game. The way they behave on the pitch when faced with their opponents, doesn't necessarily translate into their everyday life.'

At that moment, Joe and Angela reappeared. 'I'll leave you with the girls, Angela,' Joe said. 'I need a quick cough and spit.'

'Coincidence,' Tanner said. 'I was just about to step outside myself.' He stood up. 'Shall we?'

The two men disappeared, and Angela sat with the women. She was clearly distressed, almost on the verge of tears.

Brenda made an effort to calm her. 'I shouldn't worry too much, luv. You've got Joe on your side, and I know we all take the wee-wee with him, but when he gets a bit between his teeth, he won't stop until he gets to the truth.'

* * *

An hour later, at the police station, a mile from the International, preparing to sign off for the evening, Buttle stepped into Freya's office.

'Touchy lot in Sanford, boss. Didn't like being disturbed at this time of night, but I managed to speak to that DI Craddock. Turns out she's Murray's niece, and according to her, if you've got Murray on your side, you can put your feet up and leave it to him. He's the absolute bees knees when it comes to cracking cases like this.'

'I get the feeling I've heard of him before, Tom. Something in Scarborough or Filey a year or two back.' She yawned. 'Time I was on my way home. First thing in the morning, I'm gonna speak to this superintendent come on or whatever he's called—'

'Cummins, ma'am. Well known in this neck of the woods, funnily enough. Worked out of York for long enough, and he did odds and sods of turns in Scarborough.'

'In that case, if you're right about Murray working in the Scarborough area, this Cummins should know all about him. He's the station commander in Sanford, so we should get even more bottom line gen on the Foster woman, and he might be able to give us the lowdown on Jess Collier. Call it a night, Tom, and I'll see you in the morning.'

Chapter Eight

Habit dragged Joe from his bed at half past six the following morning. With two hours to kill before breakfast, he showered, shaved, and dressed for the day in warm, yet loose clothing. By a few minutes after seven, with the sun trying to fight its way through leaden cloud, he was outside the hotel at the smoke shelter, feeding his nicotine habit.

He was halfway through his second cigarette when Ollister joined him. The man looked older than his fifty years, and his face was etched with sadness.

Joe couldn't miss it. 'You're a right misery this weekend, Ollie. What's gone wrong now? Lost a tenner and found a fiver?'

'Bog off.' The other put a light to his pipe. 'And don't pretend you don't know. According to the grapevine, you were in the manager's office for the better end of half an hour last night with her what runs the Sanford Dating Agency, that Angie Foster.'

'Ah. So you've heard about Jess Collier?'

'Course we have.' Ollister sucked on his pipe. 'I've already told you my opinion of her, Joe. She were nought but a little tramp, but she were also a diehard Bulls fan. Never missed a match. That's the kind of fanatic we need on the terraces every game. We can't stand to lose fans like her.' Again he took a pull on the pipe. 'Is it right that the Foster woman throttled her?'

87

'Is it hell as like,' Joe grumbled. 'She's like me. Couldn't fight her way out of a nursery class. It's more likely to be one of your mob.'

Ollister groaned. 'Oh, for crying out loud don't say that to the filth, Joe. Please.'

'Too late, mate. I already did.'

'Oh, no. Are you trying to ruin us or what?'

Joe took a drag on his cigarette. 'Stop thinking rugby, stop thinking profit or loss, and start thinking legal. It doesn't matter what that girl did or didn't do, what she was like or not, how fast her knickers came down, she didn't deserve to die like that. No one does.' He took a moment to cool his anger. 'You know she mugged Angie earlier in the afternoon, don't you?'

'Well, I knew Foster had been robbed. What makes you think it was Collier?'

'She had Angie's bag with her when she was found dead on the beach. How else would she come by it if she didn't nick it? And that's why I know it wasn't Angie who topped her.'

Ollister's brow creased. 'Come again?'

'Angie Foster's not stupid, man. She wouldn't have throttled Collier and left her handbag behind, would she?'

Ollister grunted. 'Makes sense, I suppose.'

Joe was not through. 'What I did notice was Collier sitting with three or four of your guys at dinner, last night. Hell, Ollie, you pointed her out to me. And as if I didn't recognise her from my café earlier in the day, those tattoos were unmissable. The next time I looked, they'd all gone. Her and your guys.'

Ollister nodded. 'Yes, and Dave Drummond was one of them. I'm telling you, Joe, if I get my hands on him, I'll crucify him. And if he strangled her, there won't be anything left for the police to prosecute by the time I'm done with him.'

Joe crushed out the second cigarette and promptly began to roll another. 'You're getting out of your pram again, Ollie. Just calm down. I'm not saying it was one of your lads. It's just as likely to be some local scrote, but when you're dealing with the police, you have to put them in the picture properly, and your guys are all in the frame.'

'Aye, especially when they're accusing some tart that you fancy.'

'Sod off. Angie Foster's one of my members.' Joe eased his anger. 'You're like me, Ollie. A businessman. It's up to people like you and me to set an example to younger people. That should start with law and order, and it's where I start. And I expect people like you to support me.'

'Carry on expecting.'

'No bloody point talking to you this morning, is there?' He jammed the fresh cigarette into his mouth and lit it. 'You hired me to find out whether Dave Drummond really was playing away from home with Jess Collier. I'll need to speak to your people – and so will plod – and I don't care whether you like that or not. I've never been keen on the word "duty" but people like you and me, business people, older, calmer, have a responsibility to help the police as much as we can. And beyond that, I'll still keep an eye on Dave Drummond.'

Ollister remained silent for some time, and

when he next spoke, it was with a less confrontational voice. 'I know you're right, Joe. It's just that I can't believe things could go wrong this badly.'

'Huh? You should join the 3rd Age Club, pal. You'd be amazed at the number of times things go base over apex when we're away. Do me a favour, Ollie. They'll be serving breakfast in an hour. When that's done, get your people together somewhere, either in the hotel, on the promenade, or wherever, and let me speak to them.'

Ollister stood up and prepared to leave. 'Fair enough, old lad. But don't hold 'em back too long. We've a match this afternoon. I'll catch up with you after breakfast.'

He left and Joe stared towards the sea. Seventy, eighty miles from home, and here he was involved in another murder, confronted with a number of possible suspects, none of whom was likely to have committed the crime.

He returned to his room at a quarter to eight, having called first at reception to speak to Natalie Vallance or Brian Lambert, but he was told that neither would be on duty until lunchtime. It made sense. They were still working in the bar late the previous evening.

As he made his way back to the room, his phone tweeted to indicate an incoming text message. A view of the menu told him it was from the same number which had been harassing him at intervals over the last few weeks.

Even as he opened it he guessed that many people would be nervous about doing so. This kind of harassment was almost guaranteed to increase stress and even fear. Not with Joe Murray. Small he might be, useless in a fight he definitely was, but he had never lacked courage and even before he read the message, the only emotion it generated was anger.

I notice Bridlington doesn't have a decent rollercoaster. Not to worry. I'll put you on one.

Joe's annoyance made his hands shake as he tapped in his furious response.

Stop hiding behind text messages. I told you before. Come out and face me, you coward.

He knew that Sheila, Brenda, even Cheryl would shout at him for replying, but thinking on Brenda's recent trauma, he decided to say nothing about it to them.

Sheila and Brenda were waiting for him in the lobby at half past eight, and they had Angela Foster with them. It was entirely typical of the two women to form protective armour around a club member faced with potential problems with the police. Similar, although not quite the same, as the manner in which he and Sheila formed a protective shell around Brenda in the immediate aftermath of the previous day's trauma.

After the customary morning greetings, they made their way into the dining room, helped themselves to self-service breakfast, Joe opting for all the ingredients of a full English, and then moved to a table over by the windows.

'Any thoughts on last night and Jess Collier, Joe?' Brenda asked.

It was inevitable that even with a possible

suspect sat alongside them, one of the pair would pose the question.

'Yes,' he replied. 'I think I'm cold and starving hungry.' He cut through a slice of bacon. 'And I'm thinking how can anyone call this catering? More like cold leftovers than decent rashers.'

'Mass catering, Joe. Not like The Lazy Luncheonette.'

He scowled in Sheila's direction. 'We're mass catering but we don't serve half cold meals.'

'Joe, we cook to order, as you ruddy well know.' Brenda waved her arms at the dining room. 'This place caters for hundreds every morning, but we're lucky if we sell twenty breakfasts, and only then if we're really busy. Even some of the draymen choose butties instead of a meal. Now forget the food, and tell us where you're up to. Sheila and I were talking about it last night, and we think you could do with some unbiased information on the Collier girl.'

Chewing on the piece of rubbery bacon, Joe nodded. He swallowed it, and asked, 'Where am I likely to get that?'

'Closer to home than you might think,' Sheila said. 'Have you thought about asking Cheryl, Lee, Kayleigh about her? They were quite scathing about her yesterday in The Lazy Luncheonette, but judging from the little they said, they must know the poor woman.'

Joe's eyes brightened. 'You know, Sheila, that's the most sensible thing you've said all morning.'

'All morning?' Brenda giggled. 'Give us a

92

chance, Joe. We've only been out of bed half an hour.'

'And who were you in bed with?' Before she could rise to his jibe, he went on, 'The minute we're through with this gunge—' he pointed his fork at the half finished meal '— I'll give them a ring at The Lazy Luncheonette.'

The two women were amazed. 'In the middle of the morning rush?' Sheila demanded.

'It's Saturday,' Joe reminded them. 'They won't be that busy.'

The two women laughed. 'It's also Easter Saturday, Joe?' Brenda reminded him. 'The draymen are on time and a half and working all day today, and after them there'll be a cast of thousands calling in from the retail park.'

'Bugger. I forgot.'

Sheila pressed the matter further. 'And can we assume you also forgot that Lee and Cheryl are bringing young Danny here for later this afternoon and all of tomorrow?'

'You're right. I did forget. It's a sign of malnutrition. I need a decent feed, not this muck.' He smiled across at Angela. 'Don't worry, girl, we'll get this sorted out for you.'

'Lee, Cheryl, Danny? Don't they run your café when you're away?' Angela asked.

'Well, Lee and Cheryl do, but the place is closed on Easter Monday,' Brenda explained. 'His lordship doesn't like doing it, but when we've opened up in the past, it's been a dead loss. Still and all, your troubles will keep his mind off it.'

Angela, who had been working her way

93

through a bowl of cereal, concentrated on him. 'Really, Joe, you don't have to go to this trouble for me. I know I'm innocent, and somewhere along the line, I'm sure the police will recognise that.'

'Oh yes? The same way they recognised it when they threw me in Sanford nick that time? Four days I was in there, before they finally found out I'd been telling the truth all along. No, Angela, you're a club member, and you're entitled to the same support as any other member. Besides which, as I said to Ollie, and as Sheila's just hinted, I don't know this Collier lass. I know she doesn't have a good reputation, but no matter what she was like, she didn't deserve to die like that.'

There was a brief hiatus in the conversation eventually broken by Sheila. 'So now that we've scotched all your plans, Joe, what are you going to do with the day? Brenda and I are—'

'Going shopping.' Having interrupted, Joe did not wait for them to agree. 'I'll have to catch up with you later. I'm meeting Ollie and his team after breakfast.'

Brenda's eyebrows rose. 'You suspect one of them?'

'Wouldn't you? Listen to me. This Collier girl has a reputation for being the Sanford Bulls' bike.' He raised his hands to stem the inevitable howl of protest which would come from the three women. 'I know, I know. I'm not saying it's true, but I'm assured that no one knows her better than the Bulls team. And you two—' he wagged a pointing finger between Sheila and Brenda '— know the score on murder better than anyone. In most cases, the victim is known to the killer.' His finger now aimed at Angela. 'If we're to clear this lass's name, I have to start somewhere, and the Bulls is the logical place.'

At that moment, Natalie entered the dining room, looked around, focused on them, and carried across. 'Good morning, ladies and, er, gentleman. I'm sorry to disturb your meal, but we've had a call from the police, Ms Foster. They'd like you to call at the police station this morning.'

Angela appeared alarmed. 'They didn't say why?'

'I'm sorry, no. They just asked me to pass the message on.'

Natalie took her leave and Angela sucked in her breath. 'I'll make my way there once I'm finished with breakfast.'

Joe, ever alert to all possibilities, said, 'I've other issues to deal with, Angela, but if they start to come in heavy, they have my number so get them to give me a ring, and I'll cut along there as soon as I can.'

Angela pushed her chair back and got to her feet. 'I'm sure everything will be all right, but thank you, Joe. If you'll all excuse me, I'll take my leave of you and get off down there.' With a final nod, she left them.

Joe tutted. 'I'm amazed at how naive some adults can be. If she's not careful, they'll have her in front of a magistrate and walled up awaiting trial.'

Sheila looked down her nose at him. 'And your opinion of the police has gone seriously downhill just lately.'

He bristled. 'Think about it, Sheila. Who did all the work when Brenda was…?' He did not want to put it into words what Brenda was with them. 'When we were looking for Brenda? Not Terry Cummins and his gang, Ray Dockerty, not our Gemma. It was us. You, me, Les Tanner, George and Owen. We did all the graft.'

Brenda reached across the table and took his hand. 'And you know how grateful I am, Joe. Even so, you can't blame the police. They have procedures and they have to stick to them. Good Lord, you've complained enough in the past when they don't follow their procedures.'

'As much as you've complained when they do follow them,' Sheila echoed.

Brenda giggled. 'I think Joe's getting sweet on Angie Foster.' Now she laid a beatific gaze upon him. 'Why do you bother with old hags like that, Joe? You have me here to take care of your, erm, needs.'

'When you two are through talking about me, I am not looking to slide into bed alongside her. Like I said, she's a member of the 3rd Age Club. That was nothing to do with me or it wouldn't have happened, but such being the case, she's entitled to our support.' He pushed his plate to one side, got to his feet, and said, 'It's time I was getting together with Ollie and his group of thugs. I'll ring you when I'm through with them, and we'll meet up somewhere.'

Chapter Nine

At just turned nine o'clock, Joe's meeting with the Sanford Bulls still not organised, Sheila and Brenda left the hotel for a steady, half-mile walk into Bridlington. They passed Promenades, where they'd scoured the shops the previous day, and further down, turned into King Street where the stalls of a Saturday market were in the process of setting up.

Preferring to give the stallholders time to get themselves properly up and running, they ambled along the street, and turned into Boyes, a large department store with branches throughout northern England. Once inside, with unerring accuracy, they homed in on the women's wear department, and passed some time ferreting through the goods on offer.

Sheila chose nothing, but Brenda selected and paid for two garish T-shirts, one a black-and-white, zebra print, the other plain white but decorated with a stylised sunny beach across the front.

'Ideal for Benidorm later this year,' she said as she made for the checkout to pay for them. 'If it ever happens.'

From there, they moved up to the top floor and the cafeteria, and as they went up in the lift, Sheila asked, 'What do you mean if Benidorm ever happens?'

'I'm not talking about me. I'm sure I'll be all right by the autumn. I'm thinking Joe and his tummy troubles,' Brenda explained. 'I know it doesn't bother him much, but suppose the hospital call for him and he's laid up when we're supposed to go?'

'Well, you and I can go together, can't we?'

Brenda shook her head. 'Don't take this the wrong way, Sheila, but without Joe, I don't want to go.'

Once in the cafeteria, Sheila queued for coffee, and Brenda took a seat over by the windows.

The view was spectacular. Looking south-east, most of the southern suburbs of the town, and the whole of Bridlington Bay were visible for many miles, the sands glistening in the morning light, the sea relatively calm, the sky clear, uninterrupted sunshine beaming its soothing balm on the landscape.

'Curious,' Brenda said as Sheila joined her. 'It's called Bridlington Bay, but you can't see the southern edge, can you?'

'Working from memory, I think the coast just sort of meanders down all the way to Spurn Point and the Humber estuary.'

Mention of the Humber's intersection with the North Sea prompted Brenda's memory. Stirring a couple of sweeteners into her coffee, she said, 'Remember Cleethorpes? We were looking at the estuary from the other side of the Humber then, weren't we?' Her cheerful features sagged. 'And Joe's doing it again, isn't he? He poked his nose into that killing in Cleethorpes, and he's at it again here, only this time, he's hoping to get his feet under Angie Foster's table.'

Sheila sipped her coffee with approval, pursed her lips, put the cup down, and focused on her best friend. 'Jealous? I don't think you have any need to be.'

Brenda took a while to answer. 'You want the truth, Sheila, I love him.' She hastened on before her friend could put the wrong interpretation on her words. 'I don't mean I'm in love with him. I know we have our fun now and then, me and him, but it's not as if I'm ready to marry him or anything like that. Crikey, if he got down on one knee and proposed, I'd knock his stupid head off. That's not what I mean when I say I love him. I mean… Oh hell, I don't know what I mean.'

Sheila, always the least emotional, the clearest thinker, toyed with her latte, stirring the top layer of froth, spooning some out and pouring it back in and agitating it again, and it was obvious that she was working through Brenda's admission, and calculating a response.

She did not share Brenda's freewheeling approach to life, and there were times when she openly disapproved of her friend's carnal indulgence, even though it did not happen as often as many people assumed. On the other hand, she felt it important to help Brenda, without overt criticism.

'What you mean is, Joe is one of the most important men in your life.'

Brenda shook her head. 'Not one of, but *the* most important man in my life.' She hurried on making yet another attempt to explain herself. 'When I had that panic attack yesterday he forced his way through the crowds, literally shoved them out of the way and told them to back off. Yet when he came to me, he was so gentle and encouraging. Not at all like he usually is. And you weren't there when he outfaced that bitch back in February. You only turned up about five or ten minutes later. We all know what Joe's like when it comes to fighting. Useless. She was going to kill him and then leave me to starve, but that didn't stop him. He floored her with a couple of kicks, and then stamped on her wrist to stop her grabbing the knife again.' A tear formed in her eye. 'If it hadn't been for him, I'd have been dead. She would have left me to starve to death. I owe him so much, Sheila.'

'You don't know the half of it, Brenda. All right, so I wasn't there when he tackled her, but I was with him all the way through those days.'

'I'm not saying you weren't part of the overall effort, Sheila. I'm simply saying—'

'I know what you're saying,' Sheila interrupted. 'What I'm trying to tell you is just how hard Joe worked on your behalf from the very moment we received that first video. Time and again, the police told him to take a back seat, keep his ear to the ground but leave the practical effort to them. As always, he ignored them. He put himself out and about, garnered the assistance of other members of the 3rd Age Club, and even the draymen. And on that last night, even though the police told him precisely what to do, he still ignored them and stationed George and Owen at strategic points. And I have to be honest, I argued against that last idea. I thought it would be counterproductive. But for all the notice he took of me and the police,

I might as well have kept my mouth shut.' Sheila sat back and stared through the windows, taking in the magnificent view. As she continued to speak, it was as if she were talking to herself. 'That's Joe. Once he gets a bit between his teeth he won't let go.' She faced Brenda again. 'You mentioned Cleethorpes. I remember it, too. The business with Mort and Alma Norris, the murder of that poor man, but in particular I remember Mavis Barker and the way she hounded Joe to get to grips with Mort, and I remember you, the way you came down on her side. All right, so I know it was a feint, hiding your genuine concern, and it's that real concern which is coming to the fore right now. What I'm getting at, is the way you feel about Joe is nothing new. You say you love him, but what you're really hinting at is his importance in your life...' She hesitated briefly. 'Our lives, I should say. I haven't forgotten what he did to stop that maniac killing me at Christmas that time.' Again she hesitated. 'Is this making sense to you?'

Brenda nodded. 'Of a kind.' This time she had to pause to think about her words. 'For God's sake, don't say anything to Joe about any of this. He's difficult to rein in as it is. If he knew how I felt, he'd be smothering me.' She forced a thin smile, which faded as quickly as it had matured. 'What concerns me is him making a fool of himself over Angie Foster. Ever since we came across her yesterday, when her bag was snatched, Joe's barely let her out of his sight. I don't know whether he has real designs on her or whether he's hoping to get in the saddle, but I wouldn't like to see him making a total fool of himself with the woman. I don't think she's right for him.'

Sheila smiled. 'Whereas you think you are right for him. Yes?' The smile broadened and she laughed. 'I've already said, I don't think there's any possibility of anything between Joe and Angela.'

Brenda frowned. 'What do you know that I don't?'

'Nothing. I just take more notice of what's going on around us. You remember she left us last night for about an hour. Joe told us her excuse. She has some kind of infection, and she needed to change her underwear.'

'Sounds reasonable,' Brenda said with a shrug. 'I'm not saying I've ever had a UTI as bad as that, but I've come close a time or two.'

'Haven't we all?' Sheila went on. 'It goes with the age territory. But my point is this, Brenda. If you inadvertently wet yourself and you needed to go back to the room to change your knickers, would it take an hour?'

Brenda gaped. It was so obvious when pointed out. 'Hell, no. Twenty minutes. Half an hour at the most. So what was she doing when she went missing for an hour?'

It was Sheila's turn to shrug. 'That's anybody's guess, but I think your guesses might come closer to anyone else's.' Without waiting for Brenda to take the hint, she gulped down the rest of her coffee. 'Come on. The market should be set up by now. Let's see if we can save some money as we're spending it, eh?'

With the time coming up to half past ten,

Brenda followed suit, and after clearing the table, they left the store, emerged into bright, if chilly sunshine, and ambled along King Street checking out the various stalls, ignoring the fresh foods (useless to them while they were staying at a hotel) pausing at the music sellers and ornament displays, many of the latter locally, hand produced, and inevitably they homed in on the clothing stalls.

Sifting through a rail of three-quarter length tops, selecting one in a predominantly orange, floral pattern, Brenda said, 'Has it occurred to you that if Angie is lying about the reason for her absence, then she really could have murdered that young girl?'

Sheila took down a smaller shirt in a moderate, dark blue with white edging around the collar and sleeve ends. 'Unlikely. As Joe pointed out, if she did it, why did she leave her stolen handbag behind?' She held the shirt up to her chest. 'What do you think about this for Benidorm?'

Brenda scrutinised the garment. 'Not bad, but it could do with being a lighter colour. Maybe pale blue rather than navy.'

Sheila replaced the shirt, and raided the rails again while Brenda hmm'd and aah'd over the T-shirt in her hands. 'I think I'll go with this, but what can I wear with it.' She scanned the rest of the large stall. 'I know. A pair of jeans.'

Taking down a top similar to the one Brenda had dismissed, but this time in bright lemon, Sheila shook her head. 'Even when we were teenagers, you couldn't wear jeans. Your bottom is, er…'

'Too big?'

'A little pronounced,' Sheila said and the two

women giggled like schoolgirls.

After paying for their purchases, they found a narrow alleyway which led through to Chapel Street, and immediately opposite was another narrow thoroughfare which would take them to the back entrance of Promenades shopping centre.

'Tell you what,' Brenda said, 'there's a branch of Bon Marché in there. Why don't we give it a quick look, see if I can find a pair of pantaloons which will hide my big behind.'

Sheila agreed with a tut. 'I didn't say you had a big behind. I simply said jeans don't suit you. They were always too tight around the beam.'

'Well, they might have something that isn't too tight. Come on.'

Brenda hurried along towards the entrance, Sheila scurrying to keep up, and as they entered the mall, they found it heaving with Saturday morning shoppers.

Bon Marché was on the left, and while Brenda's focus was on the shop, she nevertheless spotted the unmistakable figure of Angela Foster making her way into Bodycare right next door to Brenda's target.

She pointed it out to Sheila. 'I thought she was going to the cop shop.'

'They've obviously done with her. Now are we checking out Bon—'

Brenda interrupted. 'Bearing in mind what you said about her weak excuse for last night, maybe we should check out the perfumes in Bodycare.' Without waiting for her friend to respond, she diverted, wriggled her way through a crowd

104

surrounding a free-standing stall selling socks and underwear, and made her way into Bodycare.

Sheila was right behind her, and as they walked into the shop, she whispered, 'Don't make it too obvious.'

But Brenda's eyes were already scanning the shoppers, and they homed in on Angela, who was looking at an array of low-cost perfumes and scents. Disregarding Sheila's suggestion of discretion, Brenda made straight for the woman.

'Angela. Wonderful to see you here. Have the police finished with you?'

Mention of the word "police" caused a few heads to turn, and Angela's ears to colour.

'Oh, hello, Brenda, Sheila. No, they just wanted to return my purse, money, and bank cards. They've done with them, but they're keeping the handbag. Just for the time being. Until their forensic people are done with it.'

In deference to the people milling around them, Sheila kept her voice down. 'But surely they don't suspect you still?'

'No. I don't think so, but according to that Inspector Elliman, they are looking in other directions. I'm still a watchemacallit, person of interest, but as I said to Joe Murray this morning, I'm sure they'll clear it all up. I'm just glad to get my purse and cards back.'

Both women nodded their understanding but while Sheila was ready to take their leave, Brenda was not.

'Say, that was pretty quick thinking on your part last night telling them you'd wee'd yourself.

Course, me and Sheila knew it was a cover story.'

Angela scowled. 'I really don't know what you're talking about, Brenda. If you'll excuse me, ladies. I have other business to attend to.' Snatching up a bottle of inexpensive gents' fragrance, she marched to the queue at the checkout.

Sheila followed her with her eyes, then concentrated on Brenda. 'Discreet? You're about as tactful as an articulated lorry.'

'Just trying to do a Joe,' Brenda excused herself and took out her phone. 'And talking of Joe, I think it's time we brought him up to speed on matters, don't you?' She put the phone to her ear and listened for a moment before taking the phone away and staring at it. 'He cut me off. I'll get him for that.'

'Probably still dealing with the Bulls,' Sheila speculated.

'Probably.' Brenda put the phone away. 'Back to Plan A, I think. Next door and a pair of flashy pants suitable for the Spanish Costas.'

Chapter Ten

The time was getting on for ten o'clock by the time Ollister grouped his players into a corner of the hotel lounge and then invited Joe to join them.

But it came with an advisory. 'We don't have long, Joe. We leave for this afternoon's match at eleven.'

'What? And you don't kick off until three? Where the hell are you playing? Newcastle?'

Ollister smiled. 'Somewhere near Driffield. Understand this, Joe, we have to get the players there, get them into the dressing room, and then there's the pre-match talk, tactics, psyching the players up and stuff. It all takes time.'

With an irritated rueful shake of the head, Joe tagged along until he stood face to face with the players, all crowded around a few tables in the corner furthest from the exit.

While Ollister took front and centre stage, Joe looked around the group and noticed that the three who had been in The Lazy Luncheonette on Friday morning, Grainger, Semple, and Drummond were sat together.

'Listen up,' Ollister ordered. 'For them as don't know, this is Joe Murray, a private eye from Sanford, and he has some questions for you. All yours, Joe.'

As Joe prepared to speak, Ian Grainger got there first. 'Private eye? According to you, you run that crap caff on Doncaster Road.'

'That's a sideline,' Joe lied, 'and I only turn up to shut up loudmouths like you and the little tramp you were with yesterday.'

Grainger half rose. 'You wanna take me on while your Lee's not here, shortarse, and I'll kick you all over—'

'Sit down, Grainger. I said sit down and shut up.'

Grainger glowered in the direction from which the order came, and Joe followed the player's angry eyes.

It was not, as Joe first thought, Ollister who spoke up, but Roger Semple, the team coach, a man Joe knew slightly. A tall, strapping man in his late forties or early fifties sporting a head of thinning, black hair, bulky arms, and huge fists. The gleam in his deep eyes said he was not one to tolerate insurrection from his players, and after a moment of eye contact, Grainger obeyed the instruction.

Semple nodded to Joe. 'Carry on, buddy.'

'Thanks, Roger.' Joe faced the team again. 'I'm chair of the Sanford 3rd Age Club, and last night, one of my members was accused of murdering Jessica Collier, the same young woman who turned up at my place yesterday with mouthpiece and his two friends.' He indicated Grainger, Semple the younger, and Dave Drummond. 'This same young woman stole a handbag earlier in the afternoon from the member who's been accused. I know different. I know Angie Foster didn't kill the girl—'

'If it's Foster, she deserves to be accused.'

The interruption came from Niall Semple but

Joe noticed the slightest of nods of agreement from several members of the team, including Drummond and Grainger.

Joe narrowed an intense stare upon the young man. 'And what do you know about it?'

Semple shied away. 'Nothing. I just don't like her is all.'

'She wouldn't let you join her dating agency, huh? She did the same to me, but I didn't take it that personally.' Joe paused to ensure his next words carried the necessary impact. 'I know for a fact she did not kill Jess Collier. I think it was one of you three.'

The announcement was greeted with a loud rumble of denial from most of the team, but with howls of protest from the three he had accused.

Drummond leapt to his feet. 'Rott told me about you. He said you just jump in feet first and accuse.'

Joe stood his ground. 'And did he tell you that I have this nasty habit of getting it right? Did he tell you that I got his neck out of the noose? His and Wes Staines's. I might do the same for you, but according to the whispers, you're more than pally with this Collier lass. Getting too close to you was she?'

Drummond rushed towards him. Joe backed off. Several players and Roger Semple rushed in and dragged Drummond back.

'I'll kill you,' Drummond screamed. 'I get my hands to you and you can kiss your butt goodbye.'

Shaken by the near-assault, Joe hid his alarm, and dismissed Drummond's threat with a downward wave of the hand.

Any chance of restoring order was gone. Joe pressed, but his words fell on deaf ears, greeted with loud and vociferous complaints. At length, Ollister took to tapping his wristwatch and delivering meaningful stares in Joe's direction.

And with the clock reading twenty past the hour, the police in the shape of Freya Elliman and Tom Buttle walked in.

'Is there some kind of problem here?' Freya asked.

'That gobby little git there,' Drummond shouted, aiming a finger at Joe. 'Accusing us of killing Jess.'

Freya turned to Joe who shrugged. 'Interesting, Mr Murray. You still believe in Ms Foster's innocence.'

'It's not just a case of believing. I know it. The dead girl was with three of these...' He turned a spiky eye on Drummond. '...gobby gits last night not long before you found her dead.'

'Ms Foster told us so this morning, and it's the reason we're here.'

'You've crossed her off your list of suspects?'

The inspector shook her head. 'She remains a person of interest. We've returned some of her property but kept the handbag until our forensic people are done with it.' She turned on the team. 'Right now, we need to speak to you people about last night.'

Ollister stepped in. 'Hang on, we're due out of here at eleven. We have a match this afternoon.'

Freya raised her eyebrows. 'Mr?'

'Ollister. I'm chair of the Sanford Bulls.'

'Well, Mr Ollister, I don't care if you're due for a cup final at Wembley. You're going nowhere until I've ascertained the whereabouts of you and your players last night. So the sooner you stop complaining and let us get on with it, the sooner you'll get away to your game.'

Joe turned to leave, but Freya stopped him.

'Don't wander far, Mr Murray. I want a word with you when I'm done with these… what did you call them? Gobby gits?'

Joe scowled, first at her, then at the team, then Ollister, then back at the inspector. 'I'll be in the bar.'

He turned, stormed from the room, crossed the foyer, entered the bar and resisting the temptation of alcohol, ordered a cup of tea, then looked around for fellow members of the 3rd Age Club. He spotted only Les Tanner and Sylvia Goodson. Not exactly the company he would prefer, but they were an improvement on the police or the Sanford Bulls.

'Looking a little down in the mouth, Murray.'

'Don't you start, Les. I've had enough with those idiots in the other room.'

Sylvia was more amenable. 'This business with Angela Foster?'

Joe nodded. 'It's common knowledge that she and I had a bit of a set to during the Valentine Strangler business, so you know her better than me. Hell, Les, you actually allowed her to join the club. If I'd been Chair at the time, I'd have scotched her. Do you think she's the kind who could commit murder?'

111

Tanner lapsed into brief contemplation. It was entirely typical of the man to pause and consider his words before delivering them. Too many years of working for the local authority where nitpicking was endemic. That was Joe's opinion.

'I'll say this,' Tanner began. 'I don't know the woman as well as you seem to think. After all, neither Sylvia nor I had any need of a dating agency. Like you and Alison, we met quite naturally. Could Angela commit murder? In my opinion, no. However, I seem to recall you saying on many an occasion that anyone, absolutely anyone is capable of murder if they are sufficiently riled.'

Joe grunted. 'Thanks for nothing, Les.' In a blatant change of subject, he asked, 'How's the magnesium business?'

'I'm getting there. According to my GP once I finish this disgusting drink, it should be corrected. It's a slow process at our age, Joe. And you should know. Your gastric problems aren't sorted out yet, are they? And it's been over a year now, hasn't it?'

'They haven't properly diagnosed it but they're speculating on diverticulosis,' Joe admitted. 'Whether that's right or not, remains to be seen, but apart from occasional cramps, I don't get many problems.'

Sylvia tutted. 'You men. You're all the same. You say we women are always complaining about our health, but there's no one worse when a man starts to feel unwell. When Les gets a cold, I never know whether to call for a doctor or a drama critic.'

Her comment forced a wry smile from Joe.

The inane, pointless chatter went on for several

more minutes before Tanner drank off his tea and got to his feet. 'It's time Sylvia and I were enjoying the delights or otherwise of Bridlington. We'll catch you later, Joe.'

Left to his own devices, waiting for the police to show up, Joe considered the brief interlude in the main lounge.

The attitude of the Bulls players firmed up his notion that Angela Foster was innocent. To a man, the team were aggressive – as indeed he would expect of competitive athletes – but contrary to Les's opinion of the previous evening (as delivered to Sheila and Brenda) that aggression was not restricted to the field of play, and as far as he was concerned, one of them had unleashed that hostility on Jess Collier.

It was obvious from their joint assault that Drummond, Grainger, and Semple were more than familiar with Jess Collier, and of the three, Dave Drummond stood out. Not by much, but considering Ollister's tale of his clandestine meetings with the girl, he had too much to lose and much to gain by ensuring that her mouth was shut... permanently.

On the other hand Semple had passed that idiotic comment on Angela. Why would he say that? What did he know that he was not saying, and why, judging from the nods and mutters, did so many of the other team members appear to agree? Putting aside the possibility of her having murdered the Collier woman, which would not have prompted the comment anyway, what had Angela said or done that would produce such group resentment?

113

Joe recalled the Sanford Valentine Strangler business, and her attitude towards him. Hostile was an overstatement. Negative would be a better word, but at the time he registered her determination. She was a lot like him. Difficult, if not impossible to sway once her mind was made up, so whatever it was between her and the Sanford Bulls, it was not something she would be ready to compromise upon.

Although he had mentioned it in response to Semple's comment, he decided that annoyance at being rejected for dating agency membership was out of the question. These were young sportsmen, trained athletes, well known if only in the Sanford/Wakefield area, and as such they would be natural targets for women of their own age. They had no need of any dating agency.

The agency, however, was not Angela's sole source of income. She was a proofreader, a secretary, effectively a ghost writer. So had she edited, part rewritten something in a text concerned with the Bulls? Joe went further. Had she actually penned something herself which maligned, belittled the team, the club?

It was all pointless speculation and would remain so until he could catch up with her. Right now he had more on his plate with Freya Elliman's insistence upon speaking to him, and somewhere along the line he would like to savour some of whatever Bridlington had to offer.

With the clock reading 10:55, he noticed the Bulls team making their way out of the hotel (to board their bus, he assumed) and at the same time, his phone tweeted. A text message. Anticipating

114

Brenda or Sheila, he opened it and read it with rising fury.

That rollercoaster is about to start rolling. Enjoy.

He felt a twinge of pain in his gut, and diagnosed that it was these messages aggravating whatever was wrong with his gastric system. He would have responded to the message, but before he could, Freya and her sergeant joined him.

'Thank you for waiting, Mr Murray,' she greeted as she sat opposite.

'It's not a problem. Well, it is, but I've been at this game long enough to know that won't make any difference. So what was it you wanted?'

Freya pointed to her sergeant. 'Tom spoke to your niece, DI Craddock, last night, and I spoke to Chief Superintendent Cummins this morning. Both speak very highly of you.'

Joe laughed. 'Tell the truth. Both said I'm a pain in the backside who has a habit of getting to the truth.'

She smiled. 'Spot on, but both officers told us you have quite a record as a nosy parker. What I want are your observations on the events surrounding Jessica Collier's killing… if you have any observations, that is.'

Joe's face screwed up into a mask of what he fondly imagined was frustration. 'Not many and nothing that would be much use to you. Nothing concrete in other words. I can't say that Angie Foster is totally innocent in this business, but I believe she is. Like many of our members, she's quite outspoken and I know from personal

115

experience she can be a bit of a snapper but you could say the same about any number of our club members. Putting that aside, there is this business of her handbag. If she went after Collier, why did she leave the bag behind?' He hastened on before the police could interrupt. 'I know, I know, someone might have seen what was going on, but even so, it would only have taken a matter of seconds to take the bag back and then leg it. I'm sorry, but her killing Jess Collier just doesn't make sense.'

'And we agree,' Freya said, 'but she's still a person of interest.' She paused a moment to gather her thoughts. 'You were having some trouble with the Sanford Bulls team when we turned up half an hour ago. Do you suspect one of their people?'

'It would make more sense,' Joe admitted. He delivered a grungy little laugh. 'But as you saw, I wasn't making much progress with them. It's what comes of being five and a half feet tall. They're all built like concrete khasi's, they're used to physical stuff on the field, and I have this reputation for fighting... I'm no rotten good at it.' He paused a moment to let his words sink in and then went on, 'Let me ask you a question. Do you know about Jess Collier's reputation?'

Freya nodded. 'We do, which is thanks to you and Angela Foster. We haven't had confirmation from anywhere else.'

'Try asking Ollie... My bad. Hayden Ollister. He's the big boss of the team, of the club, come to that, and he actually hired me to look into Jess's activities with one of the players, Dave Drummond,

116

who happens to be Ollie's son-in-law. It was Ollie who first told me about Jess, and I had sort of half arsed confirmation from my nephew's wife who happened to know Jess.'

'And are your nephew and his wife here now?'

'No. They're due later this afternoon, with their son. You'll probably catch them tonight, but come on, it's Saturday night. If you really need to speak to Cheryl, you're better off trying to catch them tomorrow morning.'

'I don't know that it's absolutely necessary, but I'll think about it.'

'Is there anything you can tell me?' Joe asked.

'Only one thing,' Tom Buttle said, speaking for the first time. 'Jess didn't die by strangulation.'

Joe was surprised. 'You seemed pretty certain last night?'

'That was based on early observations,' Freya admitted. 'The scarf was wrapped pretty tightly round her neck, but she actually died after cracking her head against the sea wall. It seems to us that whoever attacked her, she must have turned away from them, they've grabbed hold of the scarf and pulled her back, she fell and hit the wall as she went down. That's what killed her.' She got to her feet, and Buttle followed suit. 'Thanks for your help, Mr Murray. If you can think of anything else, don't hesitate to get in touch.'

'No problem.' He glanced at the clock on the wall. 'Right now, I'd better try and catch up with my two partners in crime. You have my number if you need to speak to me.'

Chapter Eleven

It was turned eleven thirty and the two women, tiring after their morning's "retail therapy", had commandeered a seafront bench, one of many in a large, pedestrian-only, open square on the corner of Prince Street and Garrison Street. From where they sat, they could look north to the distinctive spur of Flamborough Head, south over the adjacent harbour, or stare out across the vastness of the North Sea, its ruffled surface dappling the reflected sunlight, the small waves energised by a fresh, chilly onshore breeze.

Silence was the general order, broken when, without preamble, Sheila suggested. 'How about a boat trip out to Flamborough Head?'

Brenda seemed to come awake. 'Does the boat have a bar?'

Sheila laughed. 'I believe it does.'

'In that case, it sounds like a good idea. What about his lordship?'

'I shouldn't think it would appeal to Joe.'

Brenda chuckled as she spotted the man himself making his way towards them. 'We can get him to take our shopping back to the hotel.'

Sheila laughed with her.

Joe arrived wrapped up in his quilted topcoat, and demanded, 'Couldn't you find anywhere warmer?'

It was Sheila who replied for them. 'We were hoping the warmth of your personality and presence would keep out the cold.'

'Yes, very funny. Any danger of tea or coffee, or anything hot really?'

Brenda gestured across to a couple of kiosks blocking the view of the harbour. 'Over there, matey. And while you're there, Sheila and I will have mocha or latte. Not bothered which. A biscuit would be nice too.'

'Looks like I'm the gofer again, doesn't it? Anything else? Would you like me to ask them to move the kiosk a bit closer?'

This time Brenda was quicker off the mark. 'No need. Not while we have you as a gofer.'

Shoulders hunched, chuntering mutinously to himself, Joe trudged off to the kiosk.

Brenda watched him and leaned into Sheila. Keeping her voice down, she said, 'Not a word to him about our discussion earlier.'

'I wouldn't dream of it.'

'He does need to know about our suspicions re Angie Foster though, doesn't he?'

'Oh, so you have worked it out?'

Brenda did not respond. Instead she focussed on a particularly courageous seagull which marched up close to them, then backed off a little while casting an expectant eye on them.

Brenda sat forward and smiled on the bird. 'I'm sorry, darling, but we don't have anything for you until our lord and master gets back with the biccies.' She sat back again and huddled into her coat. 'I'm beginning to think Joe was right about Benidorm.'

'It would be a good deal warmer,' Sheila agreed, 'but it's history now, so please don't mention that to him either. You'll only start him off again.'

A few minutes later, Joe returned with three coffees stacked up in his hands. Brenda and Sheila shuffled up the bench to make room for him, and after handing out the drinks, he sat alongside Brenda.

'Biscuits?' Brenda demanded.

'They're busy baking them,' he said, and dug a hand into his pocket, coming out with three small packets of fruit shortcake. 'These are last year's.'

They settled down to enjoy the snack, and Sheila asked, 'How did you get on with the Sanford Bulls, Joe?'

'Like a house on fire,' he replied. 'Flames shooting out from all sides. Honestly, I thought I could be argumentative, but they leave me at the starting gate. Especially that gobby Grainger, him as was mouthing off in The Lazy Luncheonette yesterday morning. Anyway, I'd hardly got started when the cops turned up to speak to them, and I had to hang about for that detective, Elliman, but she didn't have much to say, other than they've returned some of Angie Foster's belongings. I was gonna hassle the Bulls again, but by then, they had to get moving for this afternoon's match.'

'And where is the match?' Sheila asked.

Joe shrugged. 'Somewhere between here and Driffield. Only a friendly, and their opponents are amateurs. Rugby league's not big in this part of Yorkshire. It's mostly Union.'

'What's the difference?' Brenda asked.

'Search me. Union have more players on the

120

field is all I know.'

Brenda swallowed a mouthful of coffee, chewed on a biscuit and brought debate back on track. 'So you're no further forward clearing Angie's name?'

'Not so's you'd notice. She's still a person of interest. On the other hand, Dave Drummond is now looking like the prime suspect.'

'How so?' Sheila asked.

Joe explained his reasoning and when he was through, Brenda took the lead. 'Yes, well, I can see your point, but we have some breaking news for you. We reckon she lied to you and the filth last night.'

In the act of taking a drink from his cup, Joe paused, the cup against his mouth. 'Yes? And?'

While they worked their way through the light snack, the women brought him up to date on their assessment, but neither of them purposely came to any conclusion.

The disposable cups empty, Joe collected them and leaving his seat, deposited them in a nearby waste bin. As he came back, his furrowed brow was noticeable.

'So what was she doing for the hour?' he wanted to know.

Sheila nudged Brenda, who delivered a sly smile. 'I don't really want to tell you, Joe, because I know how much you fancy snuggling up to her, but our guess is she was doing what comes naturally with some bloke.' Now she laughed. 'I like the odd, after-dinner mint, but I don't think I've ever had an after-dinner quickie.'

121

'Interesting proposition. After dinner communion. And you've never had one?' Joe asked. 'That must be a first.'

Brenda laughed again, more raucously this time. 'I'll get you for that, Joe Murray. It'll cost you an after-dinner snuggle tonight.'

'A postprandial prod?' He shook his head. 'Never. Not on a full stomach.'

Brenda dissolved into fits of laughter again, and Joe hugged her.

It was left to Sheila to bring about a sense of gravity. 'When you two are quite through, try this for some deductive thinking. Angela has been a member of the 3rd Age Club for quite some time but it's noticeable that she's never been with us on any of our excursions or dinners. Suddenly she decided to come to Bridlington with us. Why?' She did not wait for them to reply, but pressed on. 'We're speculating that she's involved with a man. It's stretching a point. I mean, there could be any number of reasons for her lengthy absence last night. But let's assume we have it right. Is it not likely that she came to Bridlington because she knew that her gentleman friend would be here, and if that's the case, is it not also likely that that same gentleman friend is one of the Sanford Bulls party?'

Brenda was amazed, Joe less so. 'It makes sense. We geared up for Bridlington in January, and I spoke to Ollie the night we firmed it up in February. He mentioned the hotel and although he wasn't definite about staying here he did tell me they had a match. As I recall, his last words were, "you never know, we might see you there.".'

'And, of course, he wouldn't be the only one in the team to know, would he?' Brenda said coming round to their way of thinking. 'Some of his other, top drawer oppos would have known…' She trailed off as the obvious occurred to her. 'Oh, my God you don't think Angie's doing the business with Ollie do you?'

Sheila's features paled. 'Oh dear. If Viv were to find out, she'd kill both of them.'

Joe disagreed right away. 'Not Ollie. I don't believe it. He's not that way inclined. At least I don't think he is, but trust me, when I see him, I'll push him on it. The same goes for Angie Foster.'

Sheila advised caution. 'Just remember, Joe, none of this is proven. We don't know for sure that she's involved with any man.'

Brenda cackled again. 'Just shows how much notice you take, doesn't it?'

The comment was aimed at Sheila, who frowned. 'I'm sorry?'

'Did you not see what she bought in Bodycare?' She did not wait for an answer. 'Stink Pour Homme.'

Brenda's comical naming of the product brought laughter from both Sheila and Joe.

'Actually, it was called Great Man, but—'

'Isn't that what you should buy for me for Christmas?' Joe interrupted.

Brenda pulled her tongue out at him. 'Ingrate Man is what we buy for you, Joe. Anyway, as I was saying, it was obviously a gents' fragrance. Now why would she be buying something for a man if she wasn't getting it on with same?' Leaving them to ponder the question, she got to her feet. 'Come on. Time we were moving. I need the ladies, so let's go take a look at the boats and work up an appetite for lunch.'

She marched off in the direction of the steps which would lead down to the harbour. Joe and Sheila followed more slowly.

'More like the old Brenda,' Joe commented.

Sheila agreed. 'She's definitely on the right track.'

Joe remained cautious. 'Let's just keep an eye on her, huh?'

The public toilets were situated at the bottom of the steps, on the harbourside. Once comfortable, Joe stood outside, waiting for them and wondering why women took longer about their ablutions than men did. To distract his thoughts from such unhealthy speculation, he studied a historic cannon standing on the roof of a tea/coffee kiosk which in turn stood alongside a steep flight of steps which would take them back up to Prince Street. A quick check on the web via his smartphone revealed that the cannon had been excavated in 1977 and refurbished for the Queen's Jubilee. It was only as he read the piece that he realised the web was not talking about the cannon he was looking at, or if it was, it had been moved from its original location on North Pier.

Assuming the women were tittivating themselves up in front of a mirror, tired of waiting for them and suddenly obsessed with the two cannons, he ambled away, along the north pier. Which turned sharp right as he joined it.

The first thing he came across was a superb, bronze statue entitled Gansey Girl. She was perfectly picked out in the tiniest detail, sat facing the sea, her concentration on knitting a gansey. Joe had no clue what a gansey was until he checked up and learned it was the close knit, thick jumper worn by fishermen to protect them from the bitter weather of the open seas. The girl was knitting a gansey for her husband/sweetheart while waiting for him to return from his seaborne duty.

In all the times he had visited Bridlington he had never seen this sculpture, so he took a couple of photographs to remind him, and then went on his way, heading towards the far end of the pier, where he found the promised cannon, which as the attached plaque declared had been found and restored for the Queen's Jubilee in 1977.

As with the Gansey Girl, he had never been aware of either of these historic guns in the town, but as he took more pictures, he wondered how come the web only ever mentioned this particular cannon and never the one above the snack bar.

His mental perambulations were disrupted by his phone ringing.

'Where are you, Joe?' Brenda demanded when he answered.

'Out on the harbour, checking out the cannon.'

'Why? Are you expecting an invasion?'

'No. I'm making sure I can defend myself against your libido.'

'Yes, very funny. We're outside the ladies waiting for you.'

He joined them five minutes later, told them of

his uninteresting adventure, and they made their way along Harbour Road which ran parallel to but much lower down than Prince Street. As they strolled along, they looked over the busy harbour, hosting a good number of small, private craft, and across the open stretch of enclosed water, larger boats; trawlers, pleasure craft and the like were moored alongside the commercial dock. To their right was a parade of gift shops and eateries, all of which did little to attract more than cursory glances from them.

They reached the far end, where Harbour Road turned sharp right to rise and meet the town end of Prince Street. Joe took one look at the gradient, and shook his head. 'No way will I ever make it up there.' There was a line of benches ahead of them, where the road turned up, and Joe made for them. 'Not without an infusion, I won't.'

Sitting down, he took out his tobacco tin and began to roll a cigarette.

'I don't believe this,' Sheila protested. She gestured up the incline. 'We're faced with climbing the north face of the Eiger and you believe that a cigarette will help?'

'It'll give me energy,' Joe argued.

'It'll help give you a heart attack,' Brenda countered.

'What happened to the vaping?' Sheila demanded. 'When we were in Cleethorpes you promised you would make the change.'

'In fact you promised you would stop altogether,' Brenda insisted.

Joe completed the cigarette, jammed it his

mouth and dug into his pockets for a lighter. As he did so, he looked up and declared. 'Oh, look. A pork pie.'

Puzzled, the two women turned and looked around while Joe put a light to his thin cigarette. Drawing in a lungful of smoke, he suffered the inevitable coughing fit and pulled out his Ventolin inhaler to combat it.

They turned on him. 'A pork pie?' Brenda demanded.

'Up there,' he gasped and pointed to the sky. As his breathing settled, he went on, 'Pie in the sky, cos that's what you two are talking.'

Their anger began to bubble up.

'Joe—'

He cut Sheila off. 'What you two don't understand is addiction. To overcome it needs absolute determination, and I don't have it.'

'Then get help.'

'I did. I went to see a counsellor, didn't I? Yonks ago. He was less use than you two. He spent too much time talking and not enough time listening. That's not to mention trying to prescribe pills I'd taken before and had a bad reaction to.' He took another drag on the smoke and had another bout of coughing. 'Besides,' he said, when he could breathe again, 'I figure that at my age it's already done whatever damage it can, so why should I bother?'

In a show of tenderness, Brenda perched alongside him and put her arm round his shoulder. 'We don't want to lose you, Joe. You're too valuable to us. Isn't he, Sheila?'

'It's the simple truth, Joe. You're too important to us.'

Brenda pressed home on his importance to them. 'I mean, if we didn't have you, who would we send for our coffee and biscuits?'

The women smiled, Joe scowled and slowly his grimace turned to a broad grin. 'You're a right pair, aren't you?' He took another drag on his cigarette, looked at it, and crushed it out underfoot. He picked up the remains, stood up, and looking up the hill, said, 'Right, let's tackle the north face of the eiderdown.'

The distance was barely 30 yards, but the incline was so steep that it meant slow going, even for the two women, and for Joe, it was a nightmare. He had to stop twice to get his breath and when they reached the top and the level ground of Prince Street, he made his way across the street against the pedestrian lights, ignored the protest of a driver who had a green traffic light at the same crossing, sat down on a bench, retrieved his inhaler, and took two puffs.

'I think that driver's just crossed you off his Christmas card list,' Brenda announced when the two women, who had waited for the lights to change in the pedestrians' favour, joined him.

'Good,' he gasped. 'It'll save me the cost of a card and stamp for him.'

Brenda looked around and spotting a newsagent's next door to a pub, checked her watch. 'Coming up half past twelve. What next? Some choccies and sweeties or a quick Campari with a shot of soda?'

'You're worrying about looking after me with the smoking, so who's going to look after you when you become an alcoholic?'

Brenda pulled her tongue out at him, and made for the newsagent's.

Reminded of the time, Joe took out his smartphone, and rang The Lazy Luncheonette. It was Cheryl who answered.

'What is it you want, Joe? We're right in the middle of cleaning down.'

'Good girl. I knew I could leave the place in your hands. You'll be leaving for Bridlington, when? The next half hour?'

'Call it an hour,' Cheryl replied. 'We have to call at my mam's to pick up Danny. I reckon we'll be over there for about half past three.'

'Right. Well, when you've checked in, if we're not at the hotel, meet us on the fairground on the seafront, not far from the harbour. Okay?'

'I'll call you when we get there.'

Joe dropped the phone back in his pocket. 'That's the kids organised. What are we gonna do for the next three or four hours.'

Sheila pursed her lips. 'We've done our share of shopping this morning, Joe. Brenda and I were thinking of taking a boat trip to Flamborough Head, but I wouldn't think you'd fancy it, especially if you have to meet Lee and Cheryl.'

'You're right about that. If we can grab some lunch in, say, half an hour, let Brenda feed her alcohol addiction, let me feed my nicotine addiction, and then, I'll maybe make my way back to the hotel, hang around there for them to show up.'

His features fell. 'I suppose you'll want me to take all your shopping back with me?'

'If you don't mind.'

He yawned. 'No problem. I'll get a cab.'

'We could meet up at the harbour when we get back, if you like. Us three, Lee, Cheryl, and Danny.'

Joe agreed. 'If one of you can send me a text, I'll make sure we're somewhere in the area.'

As Brenda returned carrying several bars of chocolate, Sheila levelled a steadfast gaze on him. 'And of course, you won't be poking your nose into the death of Jessica Collier or Angela Foster's antics, will you?'

Joe put on the face of angelic innocence. 'As if I'd do anything so crass.'

Chapter Twelve

Although she had questioned whether the boat had a bar, Brenda showed absolutely no interest in anything stronger than tea once the Yorkshire Belle sailed out of Bridlington Harbour and turned towards Flamborough Head, several miles to the north.

Both she and Sheila found the unfamiliar view of this famous landmark, riveting. The rugged rock faces, the multitude of seabirds nesting amongst them, and the distinctive lighthouses, old and new, up above them meant that the camera apps on their smartphones were busy from the moment the boat set out on the slightly unsettled sea, and as they closed in on the vast promontory, Brenda switched to video mode, to capture the movement of the seabirds as they swooped to catch fish and then returned to their nesting sites.

'Feeding their young,' she speculated.

'Springtime,' Sheila said, 'I suspect you may be right, although I'm no authority on the breeding habits of seabirds.'

The chilly wind was the only downside to what was a pleasant, ninety minute trip, and it was augmented on the return as they sailed into the sun.

'The sunshine reminds me of Benidorm,' Brenda commented.

'For God's sake don't say that to Joe.'

Brenda giggled. 'You think he's still a bit narked because I wouldn't change my mind a couple of months ago?'

'I'm certain of it.'

'Well, I'm sorry, Sheila, but I stand by my decision. It wouldn't have been fair on the other members. Besides, it won't be much warmer in Benidorm now than it is here, will it?'

Now Sheila laughed. 'Of course not. Only a matter of ten or fifteen degrees.' She laughed again. 'You do talk some nonsense, you know.'

Brenda looked over towards the beach and the town beyond. They were square on to the International, and a quick glance at her wristwatch prompted her to say, 'It's a shame we don't have any binoculars. I reckon Lee, Cheryl, and Danny will be here by now, and I'll bet you that Joe will be with them, walking along the front towards that fairground.' She pointed out the Bayside Fun Park. 'I'll give him a bell when we land.' She turned back to focus on her friend. 'Odd isn't it, the way he treats those three, especially little Danny.'

'Compensation,' Sheila suggested. 'Despite his irritability, I think Joe would have made a good father. In the same way that I think you'd have made a good mother.'

Brenda sighed. 'It wasn't to be. And it wasn't for want of trying.' She gave another naughty laugh. 'You know me. I've always been fond of the production process.'

Sheila tutted. 'What are you like?'

It produced another guffaw from Brenda. 'If I can get him alone tonight, wait until tomorrow morning and then ask Joe what I'm like. Who was it that said, when I'm good I'm good, but when I'm

132

bad I'm dynamite?'

'Mae West, I think, and she didn't use those exact words.'

'Well, it can certainly apply to me.'

The boat's captain/pilot (neither of the women was certain of his official title) made some kind of announcement which was unintelligible to them, and made a wide turn to come back into the harbour, and five minutes later, members of the crew were helping the passengers back onto dry land.

The moment they were back on the harbourside, Brenda took out her phone and spoke briefly to Joe, then said to Sheila, 'He's not far away and as I said, he's got the family in tow.'

* * *

With time coming up to half past four, Joe sat with Cheryl alongside a coffee stall in the Bayside Fun Park watching Lee and his son Danny, enjoy themselves on the Crazy Hopper, a circular ride in which the individual arms holding the two-seater carriages rose and fell as it turned, and every time they came round, both the man and his boy would wave to Cheryl and Joe.

'I've said it before, Joe. I don't have one child. I have two.' Cheryl shrunk into her topcoat. 'It's bloody cold, too. Reminds me of when you took us to Scarborough the other Christmas.'

Joe, focussed largely on his gloomy thoughts, grunted. 'Is it any warmer in Sanford?'

'Fair point. And it's not like you actually invited us this time. We decided on it.'

133

After a light lunch in a town centre café, Joe had left Sheila and Brenda making their way to the harbour for their planned boat trip, while he took a cab back to the hotel. It was a little after two when he got there, and after dropping all their purchases in his room, he hung around the bar getting into occasional, brief conversations with 3rd Age Club members (but not Angela Foster who was at the Bulls match according to George Robson) before Lee, Cheryl, and Danny arrived just after half past three.

Cheryl and Danny indulged in afternoon tea while Joe and Lee carried their baggage to his room, and at four o'clock, Danny eager as ever to take in the local sights, sounds, and playgrounds, they walked out onto the seafront, and made their way to the fairground.

'Honestly, Joe, we're grateful for you paying for the room and stuff. I mean, you didn't have to.'

He squeezed her hand. 'You and Lee are the nearest I have to family. If I can't spend on you, who else can I spend on? And you know I think the world of Danny.'

Cheryl laughed. 'Any time we mention going somewhere to see you, he's excited out of his tree, and he's totally convinced that you and Santa are best friends.'

'Don't be in too big a rush for him to grow up. Let him enjoy his childhood while he can.'

They fell silent as the Crazy Hopper ride came to a slow halt. Lee and Danny climbed off and (in Joe's opinion) appeared to be staggering slightly, as if they'd imbibed too much alcohol. Lee led his son to the next ride, Formula Cars, a small roundabout designed for children. Danny climbed into one of the cars and his father stood by to watch him going round and up and down the gentle rise and fall of the ride. From Joe's point of view, following their antics was preferable to the grim thoughts rushing round his head.

'You've summat on your mind, Joe.'

Cheryl's voice snapped him out of his dark reverie. 'Hmm? What? Oh, yes, it's this Jess Collier and Angie Foster business.'

'When will you ever learn to take a proper weekend off?' Cheryl chided him. 'Your Gemma was in the café this morning and she was asking me and Kayleigh about Jess.'

Now he laughed. 'And I told the local plod to come and speak to you.' Taking out his tobacco tin, rolling a cigarette, he became more serious. 'And me take a weekend off? Not in your lifetime. I've never been able to just sit idle, twiddling my thumbs. I'm always on the go with one thing or another. And as far as Angie's concerned, I'm not happy about her being here with us, but she's a member of the 3rd Age Club, I'm the Chair, and like it or not, the welfare of our members falls to me.' He jammed the cigarette in his mouth, lit it, and a heavy bout of coughing followed. 'Angela's been accused,' he went on, 'and I'm spot-on certain that it wasn't her. As for the Collier girl, well, like I told you, Ollister wants me to prove one way or t'other that Dave Drummond was getting more than his share of her.'

'It'd be typical Collier.'

135

'Yes well, you know her better than any of us and I can't just ignore it all.' He took another deep drag on his cigarette. 'I'm not really interested in her sleeping around, but tell me, has she always been a tealeaf?'

Cheryl's face twisted into a mask of distance and deep thought. Eventually, she said, 'Not that I know of. I mean, she was never big enough to take people on.'

'Well, she definitely mugged Angie Foster yesterday. She legged it when she saw us coming, and I went after her, but she left me standing. Understandable when you think about it. She's gotta be thirty years younger than me.'

'You're sure it was her? She never had that much bottle when she were younger. Giving lads the come on, yeah, but not tackling others in a straight scrap.'

Joe had no doubt. 'I didn't get to see her face, but when they found her, she was carrying Angie's stolen handbag. The cops still have it.'

'I've gotta say, it's not like her. She might nick Angie's husband, but not her handbag.'

'She didn't just pinch the bag, she punched Angie in the face.'

Cheryl was appalled. 'Now there you really are getting away from the Jess Collier I knew. She's a mouthpiece and a tramp, true, but she's never been one for scrapping. You're absolutely sure it was her?'

'Well, like I said, I never got to see her face. She legged it too fast, but remember, she had the bag on her when she was found, so who else?' Even as he posed the question, Joe became dimly aware that he was asking it of himself as much as he was his nephew's wife. 'I meanersay, if it wasn't her, how did she end up with the bag still intact, still containing everything Angie had in it?'

'You're the detective, Joe. You tell me.' Cheryl gestured at the fairground. 'Here they come. The Murrays. Not so much little and large, more tiny tot and the jolly giant.'

Joe frowned. Was there trouble in the Murray Jnr household. 'You sound as if you've had enough of them.'

She laughed. 'Do I? Lemme tell you summat. Summat you should already know. Lee is the second best thing that ever happened to me. Danny is the best. But like I said earlier, there are times when it's like looking after two young kids.'

'No thoughts of expanding the family then?'

Cheryl gaped and fell silent and as her husband and son drew near, she lowered her voice to not much above a whisper. 'Ask me that at the end of next January.' She took in Joe's pleased amazement and ordered, 'Whatever you do, don't say anything to Lee. If he thinks I'm pregnant – and I don't know for sure yet – he'll be filling the house with baby clothes tomorrow.'

A grinning Lee and Danny joined them. 'Cracking place, this, Uncle Joe,' Lee said. 'Makes up for not getting to the Bulls match.'

Crushing out his cigarette, Joe dipped into his pocket and handed over several coins. 'Get yourself a brew and get Danny an ice cream.'

While his giant nephew wandered off again,

137

Danny tagging along with him, Cheryl lowered her voice again. 'Please don't tell Sheila or especially Brenda. Not until I know for sure. Sheila will be all over us and if you tell Brenda, you might as well take out an ad in the Gazette.'

'Mum's the word,' Joe promised, and laughed. 'Or it might be.'

Lee and his son returned a few minutes later.

'Did you get to talk to Dave Drummond, Uncle Joe?' Lee asked as he sat down. 'Only after you rattled them yesterday, he rang me asking if I could get a word with his missus. Plead innocence for him. Course, I never did. By the time I had time, I forgot, and I know you said Ollie was telling you some tale about him and Tilly. Our Cheryl said you'd happen talk to Dave while you were here.'

Joe tutted. 'Good job it's not a state secret, isn't it? I haven't managed to speak to him yet, Lee. Well, I tried, but I got shouted down by the entire team, never mind just Drummond. And that's before the police turned up.'

'That thing about Jess Collier?'

'That's right. And if the tale I've heard is right, Dave Drummond is front and centre for killing her.'

Lee's eyes widened. 'Dave? Never. I don't believe it.'

'Listen, lad, I'm telling you what Ollie told me. Dave Drummond was seen with Jess Collier in the Rising Sun on Tuesday night. His missus is near her time and—'

'That's not possible,' Lee interrupted.

Frustration getting the better of him, Joe rolled another cigarette. 'He was seen, Lee. Viv, Ollie's missus saw them. Ten o'clock Tuesday night.'

Lee shook his head. 'He were with me and Willie Wilde on Tuesday night.'

'Yeah, early on. You were in the gym at The Bullring. Ollie told me that much.'

'Yeah, but after we'd done working out, we went to the Fettlers for a few pints. Ask Cheryl. She played merry hell with me cos I was late home.'

'And he drove home,' Cheryl confirmed. 'He'd had too much to drink, Joe, and he shouldn't have been driving.'

Uncertainty rising in Joe's mind, he asked, 'And Drummond was with you all the way?'

'We left the Fettlers at about quarter to eleven. I dunno who Ollie's missus saw with Jess, but it weren't Dave Drummond. Norrat ten o'clock anyway, and I don't think he'd have gone there after the Fettlers.' Lee laughed. 'If he did, he wouldn't have been much use to Jess later on.'

Cheryl covered young Danny's ears. 'That's enough of that kinda talk, Lee.'

'Yeah, but I were only saying—'

This time, Joe cut his nephew off. 'You can definitely vouch for Dave Drummond on Tuesday night?'

'Deffo.'

Joe was taken aback. Despite the assurances from Sheila and Brenda on the accuracy of Viv Ollister's observations, the woman had got it wrong. Not only her, he realised. He had it wrong, too, when he classed Dave Drummond as his principle suspect.

Could he take Lee's word for it? He could. His

nephew was not given to lying, not even to defend a friend. Even so, Joe promised himself that he would speak to Drummond before the night was out. That was assuming the Bulls would be back at the International in time…

'Lee, their match kicked off at three. What time will they be away from this other team's ground.'

The younger man thought about it. 'Game'll be over for happen quarter to five. They'll need a bath and stuff and then they'll happen get a drink in the wossname, the club's bar and they'll probably be back on the bus by, say, six or half past. Is it far, d'you know?'

'Not that far. So they'll be back in the hotel by seven at the latest?'

'Summat like that.'

'And then they'll settle down to dinner and… and… Lee, I need you to do me a favour, if you can. Once we've all been fed tonight, can you get Dave Drummond on his own in the hotel bar? Don't tell him I need to speak to him because after this morning, he'll tell you to take a flying one. Can you do that?'

Again Lee thought about it. 'I'll try me best, Uncle Joe.'

At that moment Brenda rang. Joe listened, agreed to meet her, and then stood. 'Come on, Murray tribe. Sheila and Brenda have docked and they're calling from the harbour.'

It was left to Danny to end the discussion properly. Speaking to Cheryl he said, 'Mam, I didn't know Aunty Sheila and Aunty Brenda came to Briglinton on a boat.'

Chapter Thirteen

It was a little after five when they met up with Sheila and Brenda on the harbourside, and before anything else there was the traditional tea and snacks at one of the range of available eateries.

While the two women indulged Lee, Cheryl, and Danny, Joe was sunk into his thoughts. Viv Ollister was wrong about Dave Drummond, and while that would not necessarily clear him of Jess Collier's murder, it left him with no readily apparent motive.

If not Drummond, then who?

Snacks eaten, tea drank, they began the long walk back to the International. It was a distance of about half a mile, but it would take a long time. Danny walked between Brenda and Cheryl, holding their hands, Lee ambled along at the side of his wife, Brenda hogging the conversation with a proselytising description of the boat trip to Flamborough Head, while Joe and Sheila walked ahead of them, and there were many pauses for gift shops, sweet shops, where Brenda and Sheila would treat Danny, ignoring the protests of the boy's mother.

As the distraction of retail outlets petered out, giving way to standard, seaside rooming houses, Sheila finally commented on Joe's impenetrable silence.

'You're too pensive, Joe. What's the problem?'

'You and Brenda got it wrong. As it happens,

so did Viv Ollister.'

Sheila made no effort to hide her surprise. 'Wrong about what?'

From there, Joe detailed Lee's account of the previous Tuesday when Dave Drummond had allegedly been seen with Jess Collier. 'But it couldn't have been Drummond,' Joe concluded.

As the International came into view, Sheila considered her response. 'It's very unusual for Viv, but if Lee can vouch for Dave, then so be it. That poor young man is innocent of everything he's been accused of, and his marriage is on the rocks thanks to a mistake. So what are you going to do, Joe? Play the matchmaker? Get Tilly and Dave back together again? Or are you just going to read the riot act to Viv?' Sheila smiled evilly. 'Not a course of action I would recommend. She'll tear you to pieces.'

Joe sneered. 'As if that would stop me.' As they walked along, he took out his tobacco tin, and began to roll a cigarette. 'I don't know Viv that well, but if I came face-to-face with her, I'd tell her she was wrong. No, Sheila, I'll bring it up with Ollie when I see him. Truth be told, I'm more concerned with this young lass's murder. Before I spoke to Lee, I was sure Dave Drummond was well in the frame, but if it wasn't him on Tuesday night, what price it wasn't him last night either?'

Once again, Sheila gave the matter some thought. 'Correct me where I go wrong, but Hayden offered to pay you to demonstrate Dave's fidelity one way or the other. With Lee's testimony, you've done it. The murder of Jessica Collier is no concern of yours. Leave it to the police.'

'And leave Angie Foster potentially carrying the can? I can't say I particularly like the woman, but you know me better than that, Sheila. She's a member of our club, and I can't ignore that. I told that policewoman, Elliman earlier. I don't know who killed Jess, but it's more likely to be one of the Sanford Bulls mob. Besides, when have I ever ignored a murder?'

'Never,' Sheila agreed. 'But it seems to me that this kind of thing is getting to you, niggling at you more these days than it ever did in the past.'

'Old age and contemplating the sheer idiocy of an increasingly violent world.'

They reached the hotel entrance, and while everyone made their way inside, Joe made for the smoke shelter where Les Tanner and Alec Staines were taking a break.

Neither man appeared to be in a good mood, and before Joe could make an effort at breaking the ice, Tanner laced into him.

'If I were twenty years younger, Murray, you'd be a dead man.'

Joe frowned. 'Why. What—'

Alec Staines cut him off. 'And I'd be the one lending Les the hammer to beat your brains in.'

Joe's temper rose to match theirs. 'If I wanted to listen to two idiots making no bloody sense, I'd listen to our Lee talking to George Robson. What the hell are you on about?'

Staines took out his smartphone, brought it to life, tapped a couple of times on the screen, and then held it up for Joe to see.

I wouldn't ask Alec Staines to decorate a

Wendy house.

While Joe took in the message with increasing puzzlement, Tanner showed his smartphone screen.

I've always said Les Tanner couldn't organise the proverbial in a brewery and the 3rd Age Club went seriously downhill when he was in charge. He was too busy cosying up to Sylvia Goodson.

Joe put a light to his cigarette. 'So what does this have to do with me?'

'Sanfordnatter,' Staines declared.

The announcement only served to increase Joe's confusion and irritation. 'What the hell do you mean, Sanfordnatter?'

'It's a social media site,' Tanner said. 'And don't pretend you don't know. Both those posts, and others, were made by you, from your account.'

Joe turned away, took a drag on his cigarette, blew the smoke out with a loud hiss, and then turned back to them. 'I don't do social media. I don't have time. I'm too busy working. And you both know me well enough to know that if I had anything to say to you, I'd say it to your face not go behind your back on a bloody computer.'

Staines took a menacing pace forward. 'Then how do you explain that the account on Sanfordnatter is in your name, with your address, and your phone number?'

Joe already knew the answer. 'It's a fake, you idiot. I just told you, I don't do social media, and if you don't believe me, ask Brenda, ask Sheila, better yet, ask Cheryl. That girl knows what I'm like when it comes to this kind of drivel.' Joe took out his smartphone, brought it to life, and handed it to

144

Tanner. 'Check my phone. You won't find this Sanfordchatter—'

'Sanfordnatter,' Staines corrected him.

'Whatever. You won't find it on my phone. And if you're still not happy, I'll bring my laptop down, and you can check that.'

Both Staines and Tanner were taken aback by the ferocity of his response. Tanner handed the smartphone back to Joe. 'If this is true – and I'm not saying I believe it one way or the other – then you need to get in touch with the Sanfordnatter, I'd tell them that someone has set up an account in your name but it's not you.'

In the process of taking back his phone, Joe noticed a flag indicating a text message. Although he couldn't recall the phone tweeting to let him know of it, he nevertheless opened it, read the message, and understood at once.

This is number one and the fun has just begun. Are you ready for the flak to put you on your back?

'I think I know what's going on here.' He said it to himself, but both men heard it. 'I'm sorry, both of you. This is a fake account. I've been getting dodgy text messages for a few weeks now. Vaguely threatening, but nothing I could put my finger on, and I don't know who's sending them. But if you read this text, it seems like whoever it is, they've moved on to the next step.'

He passed the phone to Tanner, who read the text, and then passed it over to Staines who also scanned it before handing the phone back to Joe.

'Have you reported these texts, Joe?' Staines asked.

Joe sighed. 'I should have done, but I didn't. And I can see what Gemma'll have to say when I get round to speaking to her about it. Listen, can you do me a favour? After dinner, can you get the members together and I'll speak to them. And instead of ranting at me, I could do with your support.'

The two men exchanged a serious glance, then nodded.

'We've had our differences, Joe,' Tanner said, 'but on reflection, I think we know you well enough to know that you wouldn't do anything like this.'

'Thanks, Les. And, Alec, if I really thought that about you, you seriously imagine I'd let you redecorate The Lazy Luncheonette?'

Staines was mollified. 'Course not, Joe. But you better watch out. We're not the only two getting stick on this account.'

Joe crushed out his cigarette. 'Thanks, guys. I'll shoot off up to my room, and give Gemma a bell.'

He hurried into the hotel, picked up his key and rode the lift up to his room, his mind churning with this latest turn of events. The murder of a young woman, one of his members suspected, the potential confrontation with Bulls players later in the evening, a fake account on a small, social media site was the last thing he needed.

Conscious that he needed a shower and shave before joining the two women at dinner, he nevertheless rang his niece the moment he was in the room.

'Joe, what are you doing ringing me at half past

146

six on Easter Saturday? And I thought you were supposed to be in Bridlington.'

'I am in Bridlington. I'm getting a shed load of flak.'

'I've been hearing about it. A certain Sergeant Buttle rang me last night to ask about you. A Sanford girl, Jessica Collier, has been murdered or something.'

'That's right, and Angie Foster is in the frame. Not seriously, but she's there. Anyway, that's not the reason I'm ringing you. I've just had a shed load of earache from Les Tanner and Alec Staines concerning posts on a social media site called Sanfordnatter. These posts are anything but complimentary, and they've been made in a fake account set up in my name.'

Gemma surprised him. 'Yes, we already know about it. It's Easter weekend, and the people at Sanfordnatter are all on holiday. We were getting on to it the first thing Monday morning.'

'You already know? How come?'

Gemma laughed. 'You ought to see what you've said about me and Terry Cummins. According to the posts, you wouldn't employ me to do the washing up at The Lazy Luncheonette, and you reckon that Terry Cummins couldn't keep law and order in a primary school. When we saw them, we realised right away that it wasn't you. I told Cummins that you don't do social media. You never have. And face it, Joe, Terry's known you so long that he knows your opinion of him.'

Joe took in the information. 'I know I'll be a pain, Gemma, but could you forward copies of

147

some of these posts to me? I'll have to face the 3rd Age Club tonight, I need something to back up what I'm saying.'

'Consider it done, Joe. And if anyone still had any doubts, refer them to me. Now, while you're on the phone, is there any news on Jess Collier's murder?'

'Two things. First, I'm certain it wasn't Angie Foster. I mean, she's not my favourite person, but I do know she's not stupid. Collier had Foster's handbag on her when she was found, and I've pointed out to the local CID woman that if Angie had killed her, she wouldn't have left the handbag behind. That's point number one. Second, Collier had a bit of a rep for playing mummies and daddies with the players from the Sanford Bulls. If anyone was going to shuffle her off the mortal coil, it was one of them, and the only one I can rule out – and I'm not certain of this – is Dave Drummond. Our Lee can vouch for him.'

'Whatever. Make sure you keep Inspector Elliman up to speed. I'll send those posts across to you as JPEGs in a few minutes. And chill out, Joe. Unlike the time you dumped old chip fat at the back of the café, we know for a fact that this time you're innocent.'

Chapter Fourteen

When Joe reached the foyer just after seven, it was to meet with a wall of hostility from the 3rd Age Club contingent. He rode with it as long as he could, delivering a similar response to every complainant, but by the time he'd faced half a dozen angry members, the fuse on his temper had all but ignited the explosive.

George Robson and Owen Frickley approached, and Robson challenged, 'If you've got owt to say about me, Murray, say it to my face.'

Joe response was just as snappy. 'All right, you're a fat, bone idle git who puts too much ale away and puts it about too much. Happy now?'

'You're asking for a knuckle butty, you are.'

Joe felt the first knot of pain his stomach. Suppressing it, he announced, 'I've called a meeting. Half past seven, eight o'clock, George. I don't know what's been said about you, but I'll tell you and everyone else what's really going on when we meet. And if you sobered up and used your head, you'd know that it wasn't me posting on Sanfordnatter. I don't even have an account.'

'Yes you do. It's your name, your address, even your bloody phone number.'

'It's a fake,' Joe declared.

Alongside George, Owen smiled. 'Told you,' he said to George. 'I said it wasn't Joe but you wouldn't have it, would you? I said, there's no way Joe would do anything like that, or if that was really his opinion of you, he'd have said it to you a long time ago.' Owen focused on Joe. 'What's the real crack?'

Joe shrugged. 'The filth are looking into it back in Sanford. I'll explain it all after we've eaten, Owen.'

A thick frown crossed George's brow. 'You mean it really wasn't you?'

'Tell me what's been said about you.'

The hefty gardener was noticeably more diffident. 'I don't like to say but it was pretty insulting.'

'Well, take it from me, you're not the only one, and it's nothing to do with me, pal.'

If Joe fancied that that was the end of the business, at least until he could get the members together after dinner, he was mistaken. As George and Owen wandered off, Brenda and Sheila appeared, and while Sheila appeared anxious, Brenda was furious.

They joined him and Brenda threw her phone on the table. 'You are dead meat, Joe Murray. Who do you think you are, saying things like that about me?'

Suffering another wince of pain, Joe groaned, picked up the phone, swept his finger across the lock screen, and found himself faced with the by now familiar Sanfordnatter screen, and a comment on Brenda.

Brenda Jump's name is appropriate. I've never met a more loose-legged whore in my life. She's anyone's for a dash of Campari.

He passed the phone back to her. 'You really

think I would say anything like that?'

It was Sheila who responded. 'I did tell her that it was most unlike you, Joe.'

'Because it wasn't me,' he replied. Forcing the pain down with a heavy sigh, he went on, 'I've already spoken to Gemma, and the police are on the case. They know it's a fake account.' In respect of her recent trauma, he laid a gentle eye on Brenda. 'I thought you knew me better. I would never run you down in that way because I know for a fact it's not true, and like I've told other people, if I had any issues with you, I'd deal with them personally, face-to-face. I wouldn't slag you off online.'

Brenda was nonplussed. 'I... I'm sorry, Joe. I just... just let it get to me.'

Joe turned to Sheila. 'Had he nothing to say about you?'

She nodded. 'A little. He says I'm a vicious, prune faced hag who lives too much in the past. Instead of losing my temper, I thought about it and realised it couldn't be you. You don't have any social media accounts, do you?'

'Never been interested,' he admitted.

Brenda allowed her contrition to show through. Taking his hand, she said, 'I'm really sorry, Joe. Sheila did try to tell me.'

Again he thought of her recent abduction and squeezed her hand. 'Yes, well, let's just forget it, shall... Oh God, no. Not again.'

His final words were in response to a determined Natalie Vallance making her way towards them.

'Mr Murray, I've just had a call from my

151

brother regarding some filthy remarks you made about Yvonne on—'

'Sanfordnatter,' Joe interrupted. 'I'm sorry, Natalie, but Geoff and Yvonne are not the only targets. It's fake, all of it, and it's nothing to do with me.'

Like Brenda, Natalie was slightly taken aback. 'Fake? I… er…'

Hiding his struggles with more pain, Joe spent the next few minutes explaining the situation, at the end of which, she promised to ring Geoff at the Palmer, and Joe assured her he would follow up with a personal call once he'd dealt with his members.

At length, he got to his feet and addressed Sheila and Brenda. 'What say we get a bite to eat before world war three?'

If he hoped for a little peace, he was again mistaken. Their cold cuts salad was interrupted by several of their members, a Hayden Ollister freshly returned from his team's match, and several phone calls, mostly from people known to him in Sanford, one of whom was drayman, Barry Standish.

Abusive posts had also appeared concerning Lee, Cheryl, and Kayleigh, who was described as a brainless airhead who did not deserve her place at The Lazy Luncheonette. In this instance, however, Cheryl, who was the most internet and social media familiar amongst his crowd of acquaintances, and who knew it wasn't her husband's uncle, had already spoken to Kayleigh and reassured her.

She still reserved a little candour for Joe. 'I told you to tell the filth when you started getting those

152

texts, Joe, and what did you do about it? Nowt.'

'I was gonna deal with it when we got back on Tuesday,' he pleaded.

'And if we left things like that hanging, you'd be playing hell with us,' Cheryl retorted to a muted chorus of "hear, hear" from Sheila, Brenda, and Lee.

'Uncle Joe,' said Lee, 'if you're meeting with your old people what are you gonna do about Dave Drummond? Only you said you wanted to talk to him tonight.'

Joe groaned again. In amongst the shower of complaints he'd been getting from his members, he'd completely forgotten the potential chat with Drummond. He gave the matter a little thought. 'I'll be as quick as I can with the 3rd Age Club, Lee. I don't know what Drummond might have planned, but try and hold him back for me, will you?'

Lee chuckled. 'If he tries to get away, I'll tie him to his chair.'

After dinner, while other guests, including the Sanford Bulls party, made for the main bar and the evening's entertainment, Joe gathered his people in a corner of the quiet lounge.

Quiet was a comparative. They could hear next to nothing of the noise from the main bar but the club members were making enough noise to dispute the room's description.

Joe, who had already visited the toilet in an effort to ease his gastric pain, tried several times to tell them the tale, but at every turn he was shouted down by one complainant or another, and that only served to increase the frequency and intensity of the

153

stomach cramps.

Eventually it was left to Sheila and Les Tanner to bring about some order.

'I was one of the first to broach this matter with Joe,' Tanner told the group, 'and having listened to him, and Sheila, and Brenda, it's become obvious that this is a campaign, not so much against our club, but against our chairman, and although you are perfectly entitled to voice your complaints, I suggest we shut up for a few minutes, and listen to what Joe has to say.'

Joe stood front and centre. 'Thanks, Les. You all know me. If I had anything to say to you I'd be saying it to your face, and no matter how grumpy and outspoken I am, I would never insult any of you. This business on Sanfordnatter has nothing—'

Towards the rear of the group, Mavis Barker stood, and interrupted. 'You called me—'

Joe cut her off just as rudely. 'For crying out loud, Mavis, sit down and shut up. If you listen to me, you'll learn that it isn't me.'

A lance of pain shot through him, and he gripped his abdomen, mentally forcing it down.

For the first time, someone else noticed. Almost inevitably, it was Brenda. 'Are you all right, Joe?'

'Bellyache,' he told her, and turned again to the group. 'I've been in touch with the police back in Sanford, and they're already investigating. Someone has gone to the trouble of setting up a fake account on Sanfordnatter, and as Les told you, it's designed to have a go at me rather than you lot. I don't know who's behind it, but he's succeeding.

He's causing exactly the kind of grief he intended to. And it's not just you lot he's having a go at. I've had other people on the phone complaining about posts slagging them off.'

Stewart Dalmer got to his feet. 'All right, Joe, let's accept your version of events. What are you doing about it?'

Joe had never hidden a slight antipathy towards Dalmer, and with the pain in his gut getting worse, he struggled to hide that dislike. 'Why don't you get on there and flag it up as a fake?' almost immediately, he regretted having said it. 'Sorry, Stewart. I don't know what I can do about it. I don't have anything to do with social media. I never have. As I say, the police are looking into it. Like so many other people, they got some stick from this clown, but they realised it wasn't me. All I can say is, make a note of all the posts having a go at you, and when the cops finally get hold of the culprit and they haul him into court, we'll have plenty of evidence against him. For now, all I can suggest is, please back off. This isn't me. None of it is anything to do with me.'

Still trying his best to hide the agony in his stomach, Joe sat down again, allowing Sheila to take centre stage and plead with the members for a show of solidarity and support for Joe.

Sat alongside him, Brenda had other concerns. Keeping her voice down, she asked again, 'Are you all right?'

'Cramps,' he confessed. 'I'll be all right in a minute or two. Don't make a fuss, Brenda.'

'Someone has to make sure you're looking

after yourself. What brought it on? Is it the stress of all this business?'

    'Nah. The day I can't deal with the third agers is the day I call it a draw. It's probably the food. We don't normally eat rich food like this, do we?'

Brenda sneered. 'I don't consider a cold ham salad to be rich food. What was Lee talking about during dinner? Something about you meeting with Dave Drummond?'

Joe sighed. 'Hell. I'd almost forgotten about it. I'd better get to them now.'

He got to his feet, and Brenda stood with him. 'Not on your own, you don't.'

As they made for the foyer, Sheila joined them, and Brenda demanded to know what was going on. Joe gave her a brief overview, and concluded, 'I'm getting Drummond off the hook, just the same way as I did with Rott in Windermere that time.'

They found Drummond sat with Lee and Cheryl, and they appeared to be enjoying a joke, but the player's features darkened when Joe approached.

'Dave—' Joe began, only to be interrupted by Drummond.

'I've nowt to say to you, Murray, so why don't you just sod off and leave me alone?'

'No, lad, you don't understand. Ollie asked a favour of me the other day after Viv saw you and Jess Collier going into the Rising Sun last Tuesday.'

Drummond leapt to his feet. 'Say one more word, and I'll flatten you.'

Lee, several inches taller than Drummond, also stood up. 'You'll have to get through me first,

Dave.'

The pain in Joe's abdomen felt like knives. 'For God's sake, what do I have to do to get you people to see sense?'

Neither Lee nor Drummond were listening. 'Get him off my back,' Drummond demanded.

'He only wants to talk to you,' Lee argued.

By now, Joe was almost doubled up with pain. 'Shut them up, someone.'

Even as he said it, the pain overwhelmed him, and with a groan, he doubled up and sank to the carpet.

Chapter Fifteen

Sheila bent to him, checked him over, and looking up, said, 'He's out cold. Someone call a doctor.'

'I'll speak to reception.' Cheryl left Danny with his father and hurried across the foyer.

Drummond looked down at the unconscious Joe. 'Serves him right. Accusing people like that.'

To everyone's surprise, Brenda, almost a foot shorter than the rugby player, confronted him. 'Get away. Go on. Scram. He was trying to help you, you idiot, and all you've done is aggravate his problems.'

'Don't you start—'

Brenda cut Drummond off. 'Get out of my sight before I show you just how tough I can be. Go. While you're still in one piece.'

Drummond drifted away as assistant manager, Brian Lambert, the designated first aider on duty, arrived with Cheryl. He spent a minute or two on his knees, checking Joe over before standing and reporting to the women.

'To be honest, he looks as if he's in a pretty bad way. Natalie's already rung for a doctor.' He frowned. 'Trouble is, we don't have an accident and emergency department in Bridlington. Only an urgent treatment centre. The nearest major hospital is in Scarborough, and that's a good twenty miles away.'

'I doubt that he'll need it,' Sheila said. 'Granted, he needs to be seen by a doctor, but we really don't know what's wrong with him. He's been like it for quite some time, and they suspect diverticulosis but it's never been officially confirmed. Whatever it is, I've never seen it hit him this bad, but I've a feeling this afternoon's stress has got to him. Can we move him to his room?'

Lambert shrugged. 'I suppose so. But we don't have a gurney or anything like that.'

'How about a wheelchair?' Brenda suggested.

The assistant manager nodded, and hurried off back towards reception. He returned a few minutes later with a wheelchair. Joe groaned as Lambert and the two women helped him into it, by the time they were moving him towards the lifts, he was spark out once again.

The incident had not gone unnoticed and had generated a lot of interest, some of it from members of the 3rd Age Club, and as they got to the lift, Tanner hurried across to ask what had gone wrong.

'It's in hand, Les,' Sheila said. 'But if you could spread the word amongst the members, ask them to chill out, back off, it might help.'

Tanner nodded as the lift doors slid open. 'Consider it done. And do keep us informed.'

Several minutes later, Brenda volunteered to remove Joe's clothing, and get him into bed. 'It's no problem for me,' she said with a forced smile. 'I've seen all of him at one time or another.'

After that, the two women remained in the room until the doctor arrived at about half past eight.

He listened to their account of the events, and their knowledge of Joe's medical history, then

159

shooed them out of the way while he carried out a brief examination. At length he returned to them.

'It's nothing serious, ladies. Based on your information, I believe it's a gastric attack of whatever it is he's suffering from. You said it's suspected as diverticulosis. I've given him a couple of Tramadol painkillers, and a single Mebeverine tablet. I've left another brace of each in case he needs them over the coming hours. He has a bit of a temperature. Nothing rampant, nothing to fret over. What he really needs is a good night's rest. Do you have any idea what brought it on? The food, perhaps?'

'He's been under a lot of stress over the last few hours, doctor,' Sheila explained. 'It's too complicated to go into, but it's brought him into several, nasty confrontations.'

'That would probably be enough. When do you go back to Sanford?'

'Monday afternoon,' Brenda replied.

'In that case, when he gets home, he needs to speak to his GP, and he needs to make it quite clear exactly what happened this evening. Is he under your local hospital, do you know?'

Sheila nodded. 'He has been for the last year or more.'

The doctor got to his feet. 'Then they need to get a move on and see what they can do for him. He should be all right as long as you can keep him calm and let him sleep off the current attack, but when he's up and about again, make sure he understands to keep away from whatever is causing him the stress you mentioned.'

160

'We'll stay with him,' Sheila assured the man, and saw him from the room. When she came back, she sat with Brenda who was busy scrolling through the text message Joe had been receiving.

'So—' Sheila began, only to be cut off by Brenda.

'Do you know how many messages Joe has received off this idiot? I'll bet you it's the same idiot that set up a fake account on Sanfordnatter.'

'Cheryl hinted as much at dinner.' Sheila tried to make her friend back off. 'We have more to worry about right now. We either sit here all night with him, or we take it in turns to babysit him. Which is it to be?'

'Let's take it in turns,' Brenda said, and stood up. 'Would you like to take the first shift?'

Sheila smiled. 'So you can stoke up your alcohol levels?'

Brenda shook her head. 'Nothing of the kind. I'll be down in the bar and I'll be giving one or two people a serious piece of my mind.'

Sheila said nothing. This was more like the old Brenda, the Brenda of a time before her terrifying abduction, the Brenda who feared no one.

As her friend left the room, Sheila switched on the television, carried out a little channel hopping until she found something she could put up with, and settled back for what she fancied would be a tedious evening.

And yet, she found herself unable to focus on the television. She, Joe, and Brenda had been friends for over half a century, and as she ran the tracks of her agile memory, she could never recall a time when she had seen Joe so ill. In the year or more since he began suffering these problems he had taken the occasional day off, usually when he was suffering a flareup, a situation which from a legal point of view barred him from working in the café. Throughout his life, he had, of course, suffered the occasional accidents but she could not even recall him ever having a broken bone. He was diagnosed with COPD, a result of heavy smoking for most of his life, but even that did not put him down in the way the evening's events had done.

Brenda, she knew, would take it out on the 3rd Age Club members, the Sanford Bulls party, and anyone else she could think of who deserved her vitriol.

Sheila, however, was of a different frame of mind. What they really needed to look at was Joe's hectic lifestyle. When he wasn't working in the café, he was at home doing the books, sorting out the stock orders, or working as a private investigator on behalf of North Shires Insurance, or alternatively carrying out his duties as chair of the Sanford 3rd Age Club. She didn't know what time he usually went to bed, but she did know that he was out of bed, ready to face the world before five every morning, with the possible exception of Sunday, but even then, habit would get him up early.

In her humble opinion, he needed to start taking things a little easier, and she was determined to get that message across to him when he was up and about and able to take it in.

* * *

When Brenda arrived in the bar, Rita Penney was in the middle of her first spot, and furious as she was, Brenda kept her voice down as she crouched alongside Les Tanner and spelled out the situation.

'It would be useful, Les, if we can get the members together again, possibly after breakfast tomorrow morning, so I can read them the riot act.'

'A little strong, my dear,' Tanner responded. 'You can hardly blame the members for their reaction to those appalling comments on social media.'

'You're right, but I can blame them for the way they hassled and hassled and hassled him. And I don't exclude myself from that. For God's sake, even you had to get up and tell them to shut up so he could explain what was going on. Well, they've floored him. He's out for the count right now, and he'll be that way all night. And when he's right, he won't be able to take them on. But I will.'

Tanner backed off. 'I'll see what I can arrange, my dear.'

Brenda nodded her thanks, stood upright and looked around the room until she focussed on Drummond, Grainger, Semple and Wilde on the other side of the room. Her anger rising, she made her way round the outer edge to avoid crossing the busy dance floor, until she stood facing them.

'Don't say anything,' Drummond ordered. 'Just sod off and leave us alone.'

'Make me,' Brenda insisted, much to the disbelief of the four men. 'You think you know how to play hardball, well try me for size. I'll deck the lot of you and trample you into the ground.'

163

'Listen, missus—' Semple began, only to be cut off by Brenda.

'Right now, Joe Murray is spark out upstairs, and it's thanks to you and your bloody boss.' She honed in on Drummond. 'He was trying to save your arse and your marriage, you moron, but you didn't want to listen, did you? So right now, you, and you—' Her accusing finger tracked from Drummond to Grainger, '— are in the frame for killing the Collier woman, and when the filth get here, I'll be telling them that.'

'It were nowt to do wi' us,' Grainger protested.

'And I don't believe you, big mouth, so what are you gonna do about it?' When she did not receive an answer, she took her leave of them with a warning. 'Expect the cops wanting a more serious word with you tomorrow.'

Looking around again, her eyes fell upon Ollister sat a few tables away and she made for him.

'Summat wrong, Brenda.'

'Damn right there is,' she said tucking into a seat alongside him. 'Joe's what's wrong. He tried to talk to young Drummond earlier, got a shed load of crap from him and collapsed. He's up in his room totally out of it. But I can tell you what he's found out, Ollie. Viv was wrong. She didn't see Jess Collier with Drummond on Tuesday night. She can't have done. He was in the Fettlers with Lee, Joe's nephew.'

Ollister was stunned. 'You're joking.'

'Blazing mad is what I am. You know Lee. He can't lie, and if he is trying to give us a load of fanny, it wouldn't take much checking out. A quick call to the Fettlers when you get back to Sanford will do the trick. Viv was wrong, and as far as I'm concerned, you owe Joe two hundred notes for proving it.'

Ollister took a swallow of beer. 'Trust me, Brenda, I will check it out and assuming it's right, Joe will get paid. Right now, though, how is he?'

'Sheila's babysitting him and I'll be taking over soon. I've one more person to speak to and I'll be back up there.'

'He will be all right?'

'He will, but frankly, it's no thanks to you putting work on him, no thanks to your players giving him nothing but mouth, and no thanks to the barmpot who set up the fake Sanfordnatter account.' She ran her eye round the room again and spotted her final target. 'I'll catch you later.'

'Well, give Joe my best… and my apologies.'

Brenda was no longer listening. Once more she wove her way through the tables until she stood facing her quarry. 'Other room. Now. I want more than a word or five with you.'

* * *

Joe groaned as he came sluggishly to his senses. He moved to get up, but Sheila stopped him.

'Stay where you are, Joe Murray. The doctor's pumped a couple of drugs into you, and his orders are you're to rest, at least for tonight.'

'I haven't time.' He tried to sit up, his stomach bit at him, and he flopped back down onto the pillows. 'Where's Brenda?'

'She's gone downstairs. Several people are going to get more than a piece of her mind, amongst them are club members and Ollister's party.'

Joe's features creased with worry. 'She's gone out? Alone? Have you forgotten what she was like in that shopping centre when she thought you'd been kidnapped?' Again he made to get out of bed. 'We can't leave her alone, Sheila.'

She stayed him. 'I've said this once, and this is your last warning. You're going nowhere. As for Brenda, don't worry about her. You didn't see the way she was fired up. If anyone's suffering panic attacks downstairs, it'll be the people she's speaking to, not her.'

* * *

Sat with Stuart Dalmer, Mavis Barker, and Cyril Peck, Angela was initially taken aback by Brenda's demand, but she soon recovered. 'If you have anything to say to me, Brenda Jump, say it here and now.'

'Okay. I wanna know who you were jumping last night. And before you start with any of the lies you've already told the police, we know what you were up to.'

Angela resorted to bluster. 'How dare you?'

'I'll tell you how I dare. Because I'm Brenda Jump, that's how. I have a reputation as an expert in that area, and I could see straight through your lies.'

Angela got to her feet, and apologised to her table mates. 'If you'll excuse me. This won't take long.' She switched focus to Brenda. 'Let's talk about this outside.'

They moved from the bar to the foyer where they chose a table away from other ears, and Angela rounded angrily on Brenda. 'I don't take kindly to attempts to embarrass me in front of other people.'

'And I don't take kindly to people asking for help and then taking the mick. For your information, my best friend in the world, the man who saved my life, is out cold in his room, and it's all because he's been working like hell to clear your name. And what have you done? Lied through your teeth to him.'

Now on the back foot, Angela said, 'I... I don't know what you mean.'

'The waffle you were giving the cops last night about having wet yourself. It doesn't take an hour to change your knickers. And then while you were in Bodycare earlier today, you bought a bottle of aftershave. You're giving us a load of flannel. Who is it, Angela?'

A beaten woman, her head hung low. 'It's none of your business. Yes, yes, there is a man, but I'm saying nothing more than that.'

Brenda pointed a shaking, accusing finger. 'Between you, the bloody rugby players, and the sodding 3rd Age Club, you've flattened Joe. The stress has brought him to his knees. Why didn't you admit the truth to him and the police last night?'

'I... I couldn't.'

'Did it not occur to you that the truth would be able to alibi you for the Collier killing.'

'It's more complicated than that, Brenda.'

Brenda's temper was beginning to get the

better of her again. 'You're talking to an expert, remember. How complicated can it be?'

'He's a married man.' Angela delivered the final words in a soft voice, and almost a whisper, tinged with what Brenda imagined was shame.

'Yes? And? What the hell does that matter? You'd rather be accused of murder than be caught out dropping your knickers for another woman's husband?' Brenda got to her feet. 'Trust me, the filth will get to know about this. I'm not having Joe Murray floored by people like you.'

Brenda turned and stormed away towards the lifts. She had gone only a few yards when she changed her mind, and made her way back into the bar where Rita Penney had concluded her first spot.

Brenda scouted the crowds until she spotted Cheryl sat with her husband and son, and wriggled through the tables to join them.

'Enjoying the show?' she asked.

Cheryl shrugged. 'She's not bad, but I always prefer the real McCoy, whether Whitney, Britney or Taylor, and even if it is on the telly. Anyway, never mind the turn. How's Joe?'

'He'll be all right. Doc's ordered him to rest.'

'So what brought it on?' Lee asked.

'Stress. All the hassle he's been getting. Those text messages, the Sanfordnatter business, and let's not forget Jessica Collier.'

'The Collier business is nowt to do with him,' Cheryl said, 'and I told him earlier he should try to take some proper time off. And I knew right away that the Sanfordnatter account was a fake. Bloody hell, he hasn't a clue what he's doing with social

168

media. Never has had.'

'Yes, well, I was just as guilty on that front, luv, but he soon put me right. Anyway, it's not what I want to talk to you about, it's the Collier girl. If she knew you were seeing some man on the side, would she be above blackmailing you?'

Lee leapt to the defence of his wife. 'Our Cheryl's don't see no other man on the side, Aunty Brenda. She wouldn't do that.'

Recalling Lee's simplistic view of the world, Brenda tutted. 'It's a theoretical exercise. I'm not accusing Cheryl. I'm more interested in Jessica Collier as a possible blackmailer.'

Lee frowned, trying to make sense of it, but before he could say anything, Cheryl spoke up.

'Your terms are a bit strong, Brenda,' she said. 'It's not as if she'd demand money for keeping her trap shut, or anything like that, but if she knew about it, she wouldn't hesitate to open her mouth to all and sundry. Either that, or she'd demand a piece of the action. I told you before… well, I told Joe, she was well known for having drop down knickers. What's all this about?'

'A vague idea, that's all,' Brenda explained. Why she'd steal Angie Foster's bag.'

Cheryl laughed. 'Are you telling me Angie's got a bit on the side? Crikey, you old buggers don't half put it about, don't you?'

Aware of the gaffe she had committed, Brenda laughed it off. 'There's no upper age limit on it luv, and no I'm not saying Angie has a lover. With Joe out of the picture, Sheila and I need to do the logical thinking and my logic gets a bit twisted now and

169

then.' She noticed Rita Penney taking the stage again, and checked her wristwatch. 'And talking of Joe, I'd better get back up there and let Sheila get down here for a drink or three. Thanks, Cheryl. I'll see you sometime tomorrow.'

Five minutes later, she stepped into Joe's room to find the man asleep again, and Sheila doing jigsaw puzzles on her phone.

'Nothing on telly?' Brenda asked.

'Nothing that would interest me,' Sheila confirmed. 'How did you get on?'

Brenda gave her a brief overview of her minor confrontations and concluded by asking, 'How's the boss?'

'He woke up briefly, worried about you being alone again and went back to sleep.'

'Me being alone?'

'He was thinking of the incident in Promenades yesterday.'

'Oh. Right.' Brenda laughed. 'To be honest, I was so annoyed about Joe, I never gave it a thought. Maybe I'm coming back to the Brenda I've always been.'

'Let's hope so,' Sheila agreed. 'Now, will you be all right while I take in a little gin and tonic downstairs?'

'You get off. And don't worry if I don't come back to our room tonight. I don't have a problem sleeping alongside Joe.'

'Hmm. Sleeping is the last thing you two usually do.'

Brenda cast a longing gaze in Joe's direction. 'I'm guessing it's all we'll do tonight.'

Chapter Sixteen

It was almost half past seven when Joe awoke the following morning. He suffered a brief feeling of disorientation, a common enough occurrence when he was anywhere but home, and then realised he was not alone in the bed.

A quick glance over his shoulder told him that he was with Brenda. How had that happened?

Raking his memory he discovered that most of the previous evening was a total blank. He could remember confronting his fellow club members, he had an idea he'd challenged a few of the Sanford Bulls, and he seemed to remember suffering a bout of shocking stomach cramps. Beyond that there was nothing, although he did vaguely recall some concern for Brenda, but if pushed he would never be able to say quite what it was about.

Finding her sleeping alongside him was nothing new. It didn't happen as often as some people imagined, but there was nothing significantly strange about it. What was curious was his inability to recall anything of their (assumed) union.

He threw off the duvet, crept into a sitting position, and wished he hadn't. His head spun, his stomach bit at him, and he flopped back down onto the pillow.

The movement woke Brenda. With a gaping yawn, she turned to look at him. 'You're back in the real world, then?'

'Am I? I feel rubbish.'

'You been out of it since about eight o'clock last night. Sheila and I were very concerned for you which is why I spent the night here rather than our room.' She, too, threw off the duvet, and rose to a sitting position. 'You don't look as if you're in the mood for any action, so what say I take a quick shower, and then you can do the same, and we can shoot off downstairs for breakfast?'

'Ugh. Not sure I can face anything to eat.'

Brenda laughed. 'That would be a first.'

She got to her feet and made for the bathroom.

'Hold on a minute. What happened last night?'

She paused at the bathroom door, turned back at him. 'We'll tell you all about it over breakfast.' And with that, she disappeared into the bathroom.

An hour late, Joe settled for a bowl of cereal followed by toast and butter, and during the truncated meal (he usually preferred a full English) he listened to their account of his collapse the previous evening.

When they were through, he shook his head, a gesture of puzzlement or confusion. 'It's never hit me that bad. I wonder what caused it. I mean, the food here isn't that bad, is it?'

It was Sheila's turn to shake her head, hers a wistful gesture signalling Joe's (deliberate?) refusal to face the truth.

Brenda was more forthright. 'It's stress, you idiot. Hassling with this Sanfordnatter business, trying to get Angie off the hook, confronting those Bulls players.'

Joe dismissed the idea at once. 'Garbage. How

many times have I been in the same situation? It's never bothered me in the past.'

'Not quite right, Joe,' Sheila said. 'Yes, you've had awkward situations in the past, but never coming at you from so many fronts at once... I take that back. There was Cleethorpes. It wasn't quite as bad as this, and it didn't floor you, but then again, you weren't suffering with... whatever it is you're suffering. What did happen there was you lost it totally, and threatened to resign the Chair of the 3rd Age Club.'

'It happened in Cornwall, too,' Brenda pointed out. 'Sheila was away on honeymoon, and as well as poking your nose into a local murder, you were at odds with the rest of us.'

Joe still refused to accept it. 'You're talking out of your backside, both of you. If I was at odds with you lot in Cornwall it's because people like Les Tanner were gormless enough to leave expensive possessions lying around their caravans, and in Cleethorpes, it was all down to Mavis Barker and Cyril Peck hassling me over Alma Norris, and Alma telling me to mind my own rotten business.'

The two women exchanged frustrated glances.

'What are we gonna do with him?' Brenda asked.

'I think we should buy some handcuffs. Two sets. That way we can manacle him to me on one side and you on the other.'

Joe snorted. 'That's gonna be fun when I need to go to the lavatory.'

The remark brought a naughty giggle from Sheila and a howl of laughter from Brenda and it was left to Sheila to bring a more serious air to the discussion.

'We're seriously concerned for you, Joe. It's a debate we've had any number of times. You're our best friend and we don't want to lose you. You seriously need to back off a little. Find some time for yourself.'

Brenda shifted the subject sideways. 'I did a bit of digging on your behalf last night. I asked Les to get the other members together this morning so I can have a scream at them, I outfaced both rugby players, and I got Angie Foster to admit that she is having an affair with a married man.'

In the middle of rolling a cigarette, Joe froze. 'Who?'

'She wouldn't tell me but that's where she was for that hour on Friday night. I got to thinking that maybe Jess Collier knew about it but she didn't know who the man was, and that's why she stole Angie's bag. And if I'm right about that, that could just be why Angie killed her. She didn't want the Collier girl opening her mouth.'

Joe took a moment or two to complete the task of rolling a cigarette, and as he did so, he thought about Brenda's theory.

'I'm going for a smoke, but I have to say your idea's a bit thin. Think about Friday night. You reckon that after she left us she legged it back to her room, enjoyed a good seeing to from whoever this guy is, then went out, caught up with Collier, strangled her, and got back to join us. All in the space of an hour?'

Brenda considered this. 'I think I might be able

174

to do it.'

Joe stood. 'Somehow, I reckon you could. But is Angie Foster in your bedroom league?'

He left them with that thought and made his way out of the hotel to the smoke shelter, where he found the familiar brace of Les Tanner and Alec Staines enjoying the morning sunshine and their intake of tobacco.

Their immediate concern was predictable.

'You're okay this morning, Joe?' Alec Staines asked.

'Fine thanks, Alec.'

'Pleased to hear it,' Tanner said. 'Brenda asked me to get the members together this morning so she can bring us all up to speed, but I have to say, not many of them are likely to be there. I think they've accepted what you had to say yesterday, Joe, and considering it's Easter Sunday, and a good number of them will be attending church, I feel it's best left to you and the police in Sanford.'

'Like said yesterday, Les, Gemma and her people are already on the case.' Joe lit his cigarette, suffered the usual coughing fit, and asked, 'Have either of you seen anything of Angie Foster?'

Both men denied having seen her.

'You're still nosying into this Jess Collier business?' Staines asked.

Joe tutted and blew a cloud of smoke into the fresh, morning air. 'I'm trying to clear her name. She's a club member, for God's sake. Isn't that what we're all about? Enjoying ourselves and supporting each other?'

Neither man had a safe answer for him and the

175

debate switched to the current weekend in Bridlington. Both Tanner and Staines waxed on the delights of getting away from Sanford, while Joe, well aware of the game they were playing, threw in the occasional comments on the pleasure of being there with his nephew, niece, and their son.

Soon, insisting he and Sylvia Goodson were going to church the moment Brenda had finished with them, Les took his leave, and Alec was not far behind. Left alone, Joe rolled and lit a fresh cigarette, while contemplating the tale the two women had told him over breakfast.

Were they right? Was the current Bridlington bedlam seriously getting to him? He did not believe it. How many times had he been involved in such cases? Too many to count? And no matter how complex or obfuscated, they had never troubled him like this in the past.

Granting Sheila and Brenda some credit, the fake Sanfordnatter account and the trouble it had caused might have hyped his stress levels a little, mainly because the coward behind it was hiding rather than coming out in the open, but Joe Murray didn't suffer from stress. Not to that degree.

He came to the reluctant conclusion that the most likely cause of the previous evening's fiasco lay with his ongoing gastric problems. It was time – as the visiting doctor had apparently hinted to Sheila and Brenda – to give the colorectal specialists at Sanford General Hospital some earache.

He took out his phone, scrolled through the menus and as he was about to hit the green button, he stopped. It was Easter Sunday. There would be no one there.

'You're properly losing the plot, Murray,' he muttered.

'They put you away for talking to yourself.'

He looked to his right where Brenda, Sheila, Lee, Cheryl, and Danny had appeared. He grinned at Brenda, 'My old man used to say talking to yourself was the best way to get sensible answers. Where are you all going?'

'The seafront,' Sheila said.

'We're going to look at the beach and dream about Benidorm,' Brenda teased.

'And we're taking Danny to the fairground again,' Lee told him.

It sounded to Joe as a pleasant way of passing a Sunday morning, and if nothing else, it would give him the chance to exercise the agile gearbox of his mind and run over the present issues.

'So, how did you get on with the club members?' he asked as they formed a group and ambled steadily across the hotel car park towards the promenade.

'I didn't bother,' Brenda replied. 'Les advised me to let it drop on account of how they'd all listened to you last night.'

'And the Sanford Bulls and Angie Foster?'

Brenda let out harsh laugh. 'I don't think any of them dare come near me.'

'And a good many people have been asking how you are,' Sheila informed him. 'We told them you're fine. As grumpy as usual.'

'Remind me not to ask you when I need a

reference.'

They strolled along the promenade, Danny extolling his joy at the size of Easter egg he had found waiting for him when he got out of bed, the three women indulging the boy, Lee chattering aimlessly to Joe on what a pleasant change it made to be on the coast rather than working in the kitchen of The Lazy Luncheonette, Joe trying to point out that it was Sunday, more than that, Easter Sunday, and if he was back in Sanford, he still wouldn't be working. To Joe it felt as if they were a true family, not merely two lifelong friends and three relatives.

Hadn't Sheila and Brenda taken it upon themselves to care for him last night? Whenever they needed help or advice, who did Cheryl and Lee turn to?

He and his ex-wife, Alison, never had children, and with hindsight, he was glad of it, but there were those times, particularly on public holiday weekends when he wished he had a houseful of sons, daughters, even grandchildren.

This, he reasoned, this stroll along the seaside in the company of those people closest to him, was as near as he would ever get.

Less than fifteen minutes after leaving the International, they came to the Bayside Fun Park. It had only just opened for business, but that didn't stop Lee and Danny hurrying to the rides. Joe and three women, sat it out close to the coffee stall where Joe had sat with Cheryl on Saturday, and while Sheila and Brenda went for drinks, Cheryl asked after his health.

'I'm all right,' he insisted. 'It was all a lot of

something and nothing. Forget about me. How are you?'

Her face fell slightly. 'I was sick this morning.'

'Oh dear.'

'I haven't said anything to Lee. He just thinks it's the rich food we're eating. I'll get it confirmed sometime this week.'

'Are you worried about it?'

She brightened a little. 'No. I don't mind. If it's positive, I'll be looking forward to it. I mean, Danny's at school now and it'd be nice to have another baby to look after.' She laughed. 'You'll need another part timer at The Lazy Luncheonette, though.' Her pretty face became more serious. 'Only thing is, I'm dreading the fuss Lee will make. He thinks pregnancy is an illness and he'll treat me like an invalid. Now never mind me, Joe. You say last night was summat and nowt? No it wasn't, Joe. Brenda told us you were out cold last night. You're not looking after yourself properly. Lee was worried sick about you.'

Joe chuckled. 'If anything happens to me, he's the winner. The bulk of the value of The Lazy Luncheonette goes to him.'

'He doesn't want your money,' Cheryl insisted. 'You're like a father to him, Joe. Like I said yesterday, don't you think it's time you are taking it a bit easier? Stop poking your nose in where it doesn't concern you.'

'I get paid to poke my nose in, luv. And anyway, if what happened yesterday has anything to do with the grief I've been getting, I reckon it has more to do with that Sanfordnatter business.'

'Yes, well, everybody knows now that it was a fake and you won't be able to do anything about that until Tuesday when everyone gets back to work. For God's sake, Joe, we're seriously worried for you.'

He squeezed her hand. 'Well don't be. First thing Tuesday, I'll be talking to the hospital, see if I can gee them up, get my guts sorted out. And Gemma's already on the ball with this fake social media thing.'

'You might as well talk to the wall, Cheryl,' Sheila said as she returned and handed coffee to both Joe and his niece.

Brenda followed and passed a cup to Sheila. 'Truth be told, you probably get more sense out of the wall.'

She sat alongside Joe, Sheila alongside Cheryl.

A contemplative silence fell over the table, Brenda gazing out to sea, and the Yorkshire Belle making her first journey of the day towards Flamborough Head.

'So what are you doing today, Cheryl?' Sheila asked. 'Surely you don't want to hang about with us old fogies.'

'Hey,' Joe intervened. 'Who are you calling an old fogey?'

'And I'm sure that old fogey went out with coal fires and hand-cranked mangles,' Brenda quipped.

'Just ignore them, Cheryl,' Sheila advised. 'Do you have any plans?'

'Yes, we do. While we were on our way back to the hotel yesterday, Danny was listening to Brenda telling us all about your little trip on the boat out to Flamborough Head. Now he wants to go on a boat trip, so Lee booked it.' She glanced at her watch. 'In fact, we should be making our way down to the harbour any time now. It leaves in about three quarters of an hour.'

'To Flamborough Head?' Brenda asked. 'The same trip we took?'

Cheryl's brow creased. 'No. It goes further. Somewhere called Bempton Cliffs. I don't know where that is.'

'The other side of Flamborough,' Joe told her. 'You can see Bempton Cliffs from Filey Bay.'

'A proper little mine of useless information, aren't you?' Brenda teased him. 'You should have been with us yesterday, Joe. It was absolutely amazing. I took loads of videos. Hang on. I'll get my phone and show you.' As she rummaged around her handbag, she chattered on. 'The cliffs were huge. I mean, you might not get that impression from these videos, but they were so massive, it was unbelievable.'

Joe felt his blood run cold. 'Oh my God. That's it. How could I have been so bloody stupid?'

'I say it's genetic,' Sheila announced, 'but that's just me being catty. Now what are you on about, Joe?'

'The video.' All three women stared at him. He took a large gulp of coffee and got to his feet. 'Sorry, but I'll have to go. I have to get back to the International. Keep your phone's on and I'll bell you later.'

Ignoring their protests, he turned and hurried back the way they had come.

181

Chapter Seventeen

Joe was in such a hurry that he forgot about his COPD and before he reached the hotel car park, he had to stop, sit down on a nearby bench, and get his breath back. While he sat there, George Robson and Owen Frickley came upon him, presumably on their way out looking for an early, Sunday drink.

Owen was a picture of concern. 'Are you all right, Joe?'

'I'm fine, thanks, Owen.'

'Well, you had that do last night, and we thought—'

'I tell you I'm all right. I'm just in a bit of a rush to get back to the hotel.'

George nodded sagely. 'I've been like that now and again. Especially when I've had bad beer.'

'Do us a favour, George, and bugger off.'

Secretly grateful for their concern, but having recovered, Joe got to his feet and hurried on his way towards the hotel, leaving the two men discussing the incident and no doubt marking Joe down several points for his unwelcome candour.

Minutes later, he hurried into the foyer, rushed to the reception desk, and rang the bell. A moment later, Brian Lambert emerged from the back office. 'Can I help you, Mr Murray?'

'You can. The other day—'

Lambert cut him off. 'You are all right this morning? We were quite concerned about you last night.'

'I'm fine, I'm fine. Just forget about that. I need to see the CCTV from the other night when Angela Foster was mugged.'

Lambert's malleable features underwent a rapid change. Gone was the concerned gentleman, replaced by the officious, definite assistant hotel manager. 'I'm sorry, Mr Murray, but those files are confidential, and we have a duty under the data protection act. I can't show you them.'

'You didn't hesitate to send them to the cops,' Joe protested.

'A different matter entirely, sir. The police are investigating a suspicious death, and we would be failing in our civic duty if—'

It was Joe's turn to interrupt. 'They weren't investigating anything of the kind. They were looking at the mugging.'

Lambert's ears coloured and a blush came to his cheeks. 'Yes, but when they came later, they were looking into the death of that poor young woman.'

'Correct. And that's exactly what I'm interested in. Now for God's sake, man, will you show me that clip of Angie's mugging.'

At that moment, Natalie Vallance emerged from the rear office. 'Problem, Brian? Mr Murray?'

Lambert spent a moment explaining the situation, and from Joe's point of view, it appeared as if Natalie was about to agree with him. He got his protest in first.

'I can't guarantee this, but if you show me that footage, I may be able to prove Angela Foster innocent of anything to do with Jess Collier's death.

183

Now I don't want to pull rank on you, but if you won't let me help, then you leave me no choice but to ring DI Elliman, and I've an idea how she'll react to being called out on Easter Sunday.'

Natalie tutted. 'Yvonne told me just how determined you can be.'

'Trust me, you ain't seen nothing yet.'

Natalie moved to the far end of the reception area and opened the pass door. 'Come on through, Mr Murray, and we'll talk about it.' To Lambert, she said, 'Mind the store, Brian.'

Joe followed her behind the reception counter and into the rear office. It was as small and cramped as he recalled the one at the Palmer Hotel where her brother and sister-in-law worked.

Natalie took her seat behind one of the two desks, and waved Joe into the seat opposite.

'I assume Brian's made it clear that we're not supposed to do this, but bearing in mind Yvonne's opinion of you as some kind of detective genius, I'll go along with you. I need to make it clear, Mr Murray, that you don't say anything to anyone about this.'

'Fair enough, but I need you to understand, Natalie, that if I find what I'm looking for, I'll have to speak to the cops.'

She agreed with a curt nod, and spinning her monitor round so that it faced him, she accessed the short file they had created on Friday afternoon after the mugging took place, the same file they had sent to the police.

Joe watched. Angela was pacing back and forth outside the hotel when, from the far end, the mugger emerged. He/she was clothed entirely in black, right down to a balaclava hiding his/her face.

At first, he sauntered along in her direction, obviously in no hurry, and it seemed as if Angela paid him no mind. And then, he attacked, and it was at that point that Joe asked for the frame to be frozen.

'Thanks, Natalie. I've got exactly what I want. Just to be a determined pain in the butt, could you copy that screen, save it as a JPEG and send it to my phone?'

Natalie shrugged. 'No problem. But can you tell me what it is you've seen?'

'Proof – I think – that Angie Foster had nothing to do with Jess Collier's death.'

* * *

During the early part of the exchanges with Natalie and Lambert, Joe had twisted their arms when he mentioned the attitude that Freya Elliman would take if she was called out on Easter Sunday. Twenty minutes after leaving Natalie's office, he was proven right when he rang Freya. He was sat in the bar with a pot of tea when he made the call, and the detective responded exactly has he had anticipated.

'Don't you ever take any time off, Murray? It's Easter bloody Sunday. I'm not working today.'

'Fair comment. If we wanna get technical about it I'm not working either, but I've come across something that might just prove Angela Foster innocent of Jess Collier's killing and point the finger at the Sanford Bulls. Are you happy to wait until tomorrow or Tuesday?'

The announcement provoked an instant change in her demeanour. 'Where are you?'

'The hotel. Where else?'

'Don't go anywhere. Tom Buttle and I will be there in half an hour.'

'I'll be in the bar, and if I'm right, it's your round.'

Joe ended the call and sat back, satisfied with his work. He poured himself a fresh cup of tea, stirred in a little sugar and some milk, and sipped gratefully from the cup.

It was then that it occurred to him how kind his gastric system had been throughout the morning. Indeed, since his realisation of the video evidence (thanks largely to Brenda's waffling) the only trouble he had suffered was with his breathing and that was down to his urgent need to be back at the International.

Thinking more about it, he arrived at a secondary conclusion, one which was not as encouraging as his overall elation.

The only confrontation he'd had all morning was with George and Owen, and that was routine. Could it be then, that the previous night's collapse really was due to stress? The pressure of facing his angry fellow members of the 3rd Age Club, the strain of confronting the Sanford Bulls players and their anger.

It was something he would rather not consider. The Lazy Luncheonette granted him an excellent income, but beyond that, his efforts as a private investigator taxed his intellect in ways that serving

186

drayman, truckers, the office staff from the companies above and around the café, could not match.

Drinking off his tea, he rolled a cigarette, and made his way out to the smoking area where he found Ollister chewing on his pipe.

'Morning, Joe. You're all right today, are you?'

Joe lit his cigarette. 'No thanks to your boys, but yes.'

'Brenda told me about it last night. I'm sorry, Joe. If I'd known you were that ill, I'd never have bothered you.' As if he needed to think about his next words, Ollister put a light to his pipe. 'And talking of Brenda, what's this she was saying about our Viv getting it wrong?'

'Lee told me. He was with Dave Drummond in the Fettlers when your missus saw him going into the Rising Sun. She was wrong, Ollie. I tried to talk to Dave last night, but all he did was threaten me, and that's what brought on the attack.'

Ollister clucked impatiently. 'That's a bit of a bugger. I had a call from our lass this morning. Tilly's in labour. Looks like I'll be a grandad before the day's out.'

'And does Dave know?'

The other shook his head. 'I haven't told him, but based on what you're saying, I think he has a right to know. Trouble is, Joe, if I tell him, he'll want to shoot off home right away. Will the police let him, do you think?'

'I shouldn't think so. Thing is, Ollie other matters have come to light. I can't swear that I have this nailed on but I do know it wasn't the Jess

Collier woman who mugged Angie Foster. To be honest, I think it might have been one of your boys. I'm waiting for DI Elliman, and if she feels the same, there's no way that she'll let him make his way home.'

As Joe delivered the message, Ollister's features paled. 'One of ours? Who?'

Joe shrugged, took another drag on his cigarette. 'That's the sixty-four dollar question.' He paused, carefully calculating his next words. 'There is something else I need to speak to you about.'

'Go ahead. You know me. No delicate ears.'

Joe chuckled. 'Unless it's to do with the Bulls.' He became more serious. 'We've learned that Angie Foster is involved with a married man, and the suspicion is, again, that it's one of your crowd.'

Ollister took the accusation in his stride. 'It wouldn't surprise me, but don't you look at me like that, Joe Murray. I'll swear on the soul of my new grandchild that I have never strayed since Viv and I first met.'

Joe accepted the admission. He'd always felt that Ollister was not the kind to become involved in an affair. 'You've no idea who?'

'None at all. But if I hear any whispers, I'll let you know. For now, I owe you two hundred quid. Can I straighten you up when we get back to Sanford?'

Joe took a final draw on the cigarette, and stubbed it out. 'No rush but don't forget, because I won't.'

From there, Joe made way to his room where he collected his laptop, and then returned to the hotel bar, ordered fresh tea, and with the laptop booted up and at the ready, he chose a table close to the windows from where he could watch for the police arriving.

He did not have long to wait before Freya's VW saloon pulled into a parking space outside the entrance and she and her sergeant climbed out. A few minutes later, the two officers joined Joe in the bar.

'Good to see you both,' Joe teased. 'Enjoying your Easter break, are you?'

'Cut the sarcasm,' Freya ordered. 'Where's this supposed evidence?'

He brought the laptop from hibernation, inserted the memory stick Natalie had prepared for him and called up the single image she had saved on it. He turned the computer to face the two police officers.

Freya's annoyance came to the fore. 'We've already seen this. It's from the CCTV footage the hotel gave our people after the mugging. It proves nothing and you're this close to a charge of wasting police time.' She pinched her finger and thumb close together.

'I've seen it before, too, only I saw it for real rather than on camera, and the truth didn't dawn on me then. Tell me something. How tall was Jess Collier?'

Both officers remained puzzled.

Buttle answered. 'I reckon about the same height as you. Five and half feet, give or take.'

'In other words about the same height as Angie Foster. Now look at the picture again and tell me how tall you think the mugger is?'

They focused on the image again and it was clear that the attacker was head and shoulders taller than Angela.

'I'd guess he's about six-four, six-five,' Joe said, 'and that means there's no way Jess Collier attacked Angie, which then begs the question, why would Angie go after Jess? How did Jess get hold of that handbag and how would Angie know she had it?'

Silence fell while both officers studied the image.

Eventually Freya sat back and said, 'I can see your point of view, but in fact, you've proven nothing other than Jess did not steal Ms Foster's handbag.'

'I never said I'd proved it. I said I *might have* proved it.'

'Y'see,' Buttle began, 'no matter who mugged the Foster woman, we come up against the same problem. All right it wasn't Collier, but even if it had been, how would Foster know that Collier had her bag? She never gave any indication to our people that she knew her attacker. Did she say anything to you?'

'No, she didn't. However, we do have information on her whereabouts during the timeframe of Jess's death.' Joe fixed Freya's eye. 'She lied to you on Friday night. Yes, and she lied to us too.'

'Lied in what way?' Freya asked.

'When she said she'd wet her pants. Our information is she was actually getting up close and personal with some bloke. If that's so – and she's part confirmed it to my friend, Brenda Jump – he can testify to her whereabouts at the time of Jess's killing.'

'And who is he?'

'Brenda pushed her on the same question, but Angie wouldn't say.'

Freya almost leapt from her seat. 'She'll bloody well tell me. Where is she? Do you know?'

'Haven't seen her all morning. Mind, it's not as if I've been looking for her.' Joe took out his phone, called up Angela's number and hit the connect button. Almost immediately, he ended the call. 'Straight to voicemail.'

This time Freya did stand, followed by Buttle, and as they marched off towards reception, Joe tagged along.

'Angela Foster,' Freya demanded of Natalie. 'Have you seen anything of her?'

'It's not Accomplus policy to monitor our guests' movements, Inspector, but as it happens, I saw her in the bar earlier with Mr Ollister and Mr Semple.' She turned to examine the keyboard behind her. 'She must be in her room. Her key hasn't been handed in.'

Freya nodded her thanks. 'Room number?'

'Two one six.'

With Joe behind them, the two police officers made for the lifts, rode up to the second floor, and a minute or two later, hammered on the door of room 216. No response. Buttle rapped on the door again and still there was no answer.

Freya took out her phone, rang reception, and

when Natalie answered, demanded, 'Bring me a pass key to room 216... I don't want any argument. We're getting no answer and for all we know the woman could be in some kind of trouble... We'll wait here.'

While waiting for Natalie or one of her staff to arrive, Freya turned on Joe. 'What are you doing here, Mr Murray?'

Joe gave her a sly smile. 'I'm looking after the interests of one of my members.'

A porter arrived with the pass key, flashed it before the electronic lock, pushed the door open, and stood back to let the police enter. Unwilling to be left behind, Joe followed them into the room and stopped dead.

Laid on her back on the bed, Angela had been badly beaten. Her face was a mass of bruises, both lips were burst, blood had trickled down onto the white, linen pillow slips. She wore only a slip, which was torn off at one shoulder, and which had ridden up above her knees.

Joe turned away, memories of the Sanford Valentine strangler flooding his mind. That maniac had left his victims with their underwear on display, and then, as now, Joe found it disgusting, demeaning, disrespectful to the victims and to women in general, more so in Angela's case because she wore nothing beneath the slip. It was as if this lunatic summed her up as no more than the area between her thighs.

Freya rushed to her, pressed a hand against her neck. Taking out her phone, she said, 'She's alive.'

Joe felt a flood of relief as Freya carried on

speaking into the phone.

She spoke into the phone. 'DI Elliman. I need an ambulance and paramedics to the International Hotel, room 216. Female, early to mid-50s, badly beaten… No, she's alive but needs urgent attention. Beyond that, I want a CSI team out here ready to start work on the room the minute we've sorted the woman out.'

Chapter Eighteen

While Freya was talking into her phone, Buttle circled the bed, using his smartphone to take photographs from various angles, and Joe, hovering in the background, spotted Angela's phone on the dresser at the foot of the bed.

He picked it up, slid his finger over the lock screen, and picked up no less than three unanswered calls. One was, obviously, from him, the other two were from someone whose initials were CS. It meant little or nothing to Joe, but when he checked her call record there were umpteen calls to and from that number. He realised right away that this individual must be her unnamed lover, and try as he might, he could not think of anyone in the Sanford Bulls party with those initials.

'What the hell do you think you're playing at, Murray?'

Freya's voice brought him back to reality. He rounded on her. 'First, it's either Joe or Mr Murray, not Murray. Second, I was checking her phone to see who might have been ringing her. And if you're worried that it might have my dabs all over her phone, get in touch with Sanford. They've got my prints on record.' He handed the phone to her. 'An awful lot of calls from somebody with the initials CS. It means nothing to me.'

'The mystery lover,' Buttle observed. 'Not one of the Bulls players?'

'Not one that I can think of.'

'Right.' Freya took control. 'I'm sorry, Mr Murray—' she stressed the word "Mister", '— but we need you out of here. Don't worry about Angela. We'll look after her until the paramedics get here.'

'Yeah, no problem, but can you do me a favour? Keep me updated on her situation.' Before Freya could protest, he pressed on, 'Angie is one of our members, I'm the Chair of the club, and it's my responsibility to bring the members up to snuff.'

Freya backed down. 'Okay. I'll do that. We'll be here for a good while anyway.' She turned to her sergeant. 'Tom, go with Mr Murray and speak to Hayden Ollister. Make sure he knows that none of his people can go anywhere until we've spoken to them.'

The two men acquiesced and made their way along the corridor to the lifts.

'Bit of a bummer for you, this, huh?' Buttle commented as he called the lift. 'One of your people battered like that.'

'We've had worse,' Joe said. 'Filey a year or three back. One of our members was murdered. And not long after that, my girlfriend was murdered and I had some nutter chasing me all over Majorca determined to shine me on.'

Buttle smiled as he stepped into the lift. 'You don't make joining your club sound attractive, mate.'

Joe returned the humour with a broad grin. 'It gets worse; I've been accused of murder twice.'

'We know. Your niece told us all about it.' As they reached the ground floor and stepped out, Buttle became more serious. 'Listen, Joe, I don't want you to think I'm hassling, but is it possible one of your club members did this to her?'

Joe was definite. 'No chance. It's called the 3rd Age Club for a reason. We don't have anyone under the age of fifty, and all right, I know there are people of that age who like to dole out the knuckle butties, but not amongst our people. We work for each other, Tom. It's a mutual support group, and if it was one of them, which it isn't, we'd have no hesitation in handing him over to you. But I'll tell you what I'll do. Like I told your boss, I'll have to let the members know what's happened, and while I'm at it, I'll pull those people who knew Angie best, and suss them out for you. For now, you're better off looking at the Sanford Bulls. We don't know who she was sleeping with, but the suspicion is it's one of them.'

'Fair enough. I'll let Freya know you're on the case. I'll speak to this Ollister sort and see what he can tell me.'

'Yeah, well, I don't wanna lead you, but your favourites are Dave Drummond and Ian Grainger, but you'll be meeting a brick wall. Drummond's wife is in labour as we speak and he's likely to want to get off home to Sanford. As for Grainger, well, he's a mouthpiece and none too friendly with anyone.'

'I'll bear it in mind. Thanks, mate.'

They parted company in the foyer, Buttle in search of Ollister, Joe heading for the smoke area outside. Once there, he rolled a cigarette, lit up, and then debated whether to call Sheila or Brenda. Notwithstanding her improvement over the last weeks, and more so over the last twenty-four hours, he wasn't willing to risk upsetting Brenda, so he chose Sheila.

'Everything all right, Joe?' she asked.

'Not so's you'd notice,' he said and went on to tell her what had happened. He concluded by saying, 'I'll let you pass it on to Brenda. You're more tactful than me. To be honest, I could do with you back here so we can get the members together.'

'Difficult,' Sheila admitted. 'Right now, we're north of Flamborough Head and looking at Bempton Cliffs.'

'Oh. So you decided to go with Lee and Cheryl?'

'It's a pleasant and interesting way of passing the time, Joe.'

'If you say so. I'll see if I can pin down Les, Alec, or George and Owen. When will you be back?'

'About half past one.'

'In that case, I'll see you then.'

With no other members of the club in sight, he rang Les Tanner and told him the news, adding, 'If you see any of our people out and about, Les, give them the nod. I could do with speaking to everyone if it's possible.'

'Might be better to wait until just before or just after dinner, Joe. At least they'll all be in the hotel by then.'

'Good point. And by then I should have an update on Angela's situation. All right, Les, I'll catch you later.'

At a loose end, unwilling to wander far from

the hotel, he rolled a second cigarette, lit up and focussed on the initials CS, which he'd found on Angela's phone. Running through a mental inventory of the Sanford Bulls party, he could find no one who fitted the bill, and from a personal point of view, he knew of no one with those initials. Well, he did. Christoper Standish, the eldest son of draymen Barry Standish, but Chris was not yet 30 years old and unlikely to be Angela's lover. Anyway, according to Joe's information, the man lived and worked in the Leeds/Bradford area. If he had a lover of any description, it was unlikely to be a woman almost twice his age and living in a town twenty miles away.

Taking on board Sheila's analysis of Angela's absence on every 3rd Age Club outing, her non-attendance at the weekly disco, and her attendance at the Bulls' Saturday game, he came to the same conclusion as Sheila, the same conclusion he had delivered to Ollister earlier in the day. The lover was one of the Sanford Bulls crowd.

An ambulance hurtled into the car park, came to a halt outside the main entrance, and two paramedics hurried into the building.

The sight reminded Joe of the mess the attacker had made of Angela, and that sent his thinking in a different direction. What had gone wrong that the man had seen fit to beat her so badly?

Joe was no stranger to casual, as-and-when-we-feel-like-it relationships. Look at his on-off episodes with Brenda. Prior to her abduction it was once in a blue moon. And she was not the only woman in his life. He'd had an ongoing affair – for want of a better word – with Mitch MacKechnie, a film producer he'd met in Inverness. It lasted quite some time but ended with a degree of disappointment the previous Christmas. She made the decision after he let her down. He didn't take it to heart. He didn't turn on the woman. To him, it was all part and parcel of life for the single man/woman.

'You didn't knock hell out of her, Joe,' he muttered to himself.

The minutes passed, he smoked and smoked, wrangling his intellect in an effort to pin down the hidden man who had carried out this vicious – and as far as Joe was concerned – unwarranted attack.

His favourites were Drummond and Grainger, but that did not square with the notion of lovers. Angela was in her fifties, the two Bulls players were not yet thirty years of age. He could see Angela perhaps looking for a younger man, a "toyboy" to coin the modern idiom, but he could not imagine either of the players seeking out an older woman, especially when they had groupies like Jess Collier hovering on the fringes.

It was then that a fresh idea occurred to him. He'd assumed that the lover had done this to Angela. Suppose it wasn't? Suppose it was Drummond or Grainger, extracting revenge for the killing of Jess Collier? The more he thought about it, the more it made sense. What was it Niall Semple said at the caustic confrontation the previous morning? *If it's Foster, she deserves to be accused.* He, like his teammates, was convinced that Angela had killed Jess.

199

His anger began to rise once more. Those two, Drummond and Grainger, and the rest of the Bulls team were going to get more than a piece of his mind when he saw them next, and there was no better place to start than Hayden "I don't believe it" Ollister.

He crushed out his cigarette, turned and glanced into the bar. No go. Ollister was still with Sergeant Buttle, and appeared to be protesting at what he probably considered the high-handed attitude of the police. Buttle was giving as good as he got, too. Well, Joe could wait, and the longer he waited, the angrier he would become, and Ollister and his party would crumble under that anger.

He did not have long to wait. As he looked at the pair, Buttle got to his feet and with much finger pointing left Ollister with an obvious warning. The Chair of the Bulls glowered after the police officer, then his angry eyes fell on Joe. He leapt to his feet and marched to the hotel foyer.

Determined not to be trodden on, Joe rolled yet another cigarette and put a light to it as Ollister burst out of the building and bore down on him.

'Do you know how much trouble you're causing, Murray?'

Joe responded in kind. 'Do you know how much control you don't have over that gang of thugs you call a rugby team?'

'They're not thugs. They're highly trained athletes.'

'And I'm a cordon bleu chef. Grow up, Ollie. Someone's beaten Angie Foster black and blue, and your boys are the favourites. I'll go further than that.

Your bloody son-in-law, Dave Drummond, is leading the field, and that other clown, Grainger, isn't far behind.'

'I'm not having that. Neither of those boys would…'

He trailed off as the paramedics came out of the hotel, guiding a gurney upon which lay the prone figure of Angela Foster.

She was covered, but her face was plain to see, and when Ollister looked at her, his colour drained.

Joe left the smoke shelter, crossed a few yards to the rear of the ambulance as the paramedics opened the doors, and let the ramp down.

Angela was conscious, just one eye half open. She tried to smile, but it turned to a wince.

'Can you talk?' Joe asked.

She shook her head.

'But you do know who did this, don't you?'

Once again she shook her head.

Joe patted her on the arm. 'You take it easy, girl. We'll make some kind of arrangement for getting you home.' He turned to the female paramedic. 'Where are you taking her?'

'Bridlington Urgent Treatment Centre. Depending on what they say, she may need moving to Scarborough General.'

Joe came away, and allowed them to get on with their work. Notwithstanding his gentility when speaking to Angela, his anger was rising once more, and he vented it on Ollister.

'If one of your boys did this to her, I'll be in court and I'll see them in a hell.'

The Chair of the Sanford Bulls was suddenly a

different man. 'You and me both, and if it is Dave Drummond, there won't be much left for the police by the time I'm done with him.'

He wandered off back into the hotel, shoulders slumped, a beaten man, and as he disappeared, so Freya and Tom Buttle came out.

Joe collared them immediately. 'I just asked Angela and she says she doesn't know who hit her, so what can you tell me?'

'She knows, Joe. According to the paramedics, she has no injures to the rear, so she was facing her attacker,' Freya said. 'She's a hell of a mess. The paramedics have cleaned her up a little and they don't think there's any serious, permanent damage, but they're taking her to the urgent treatment centre off Bessingby Road. They'll give her a good once over, and decide whether or not she needs hospitalisation. Don't worry about it, Joe. I'll make sure you're kept informed.'

Joe noticed that suddenly that he was "Joe", not "Murray", not "Mr Murray". 'Thanks. I've already put the word out to one or two of our members. I'll be speaking to my people tonight either before or after dinner. In the meantime, if I can turn up anything else, I'll give you a bell.'

Chapter Nineteen

It was a little after half past one when Sheila, Brenda, Lee, Cheryl, and Danny got back to the International, and right away, they pressed Joe for information.

'It's not pretty and it might put you off your dinner, so what say we grab a bite to eat in the hotel dining room before I bring you up to speed?'

They agreed, and just before two in the afternoon, the maître d'hotel showed them to a table. In common with most Accomplus hotels, Sunday lunch was the traditional roast beef, Yorkshire puddings, roast potatoes, and a selection of vegetables. The five adults tucked in, but Danny appeared to have lost his appetite.

'Too many sweets and too much ice cream while we were out on that boat,' Cheryl said.

Throughout the meal, Joe evaded their attempts to push him on the morning's events, other than to tell them that Angela was in a bad way, but her injuries were not life-threatening, and she was receiving the correct level of care.

'How are we going to get her home, Joe?' Brenda demanded. 'If she's that bad, she won't want to come home on the bus.'

'I've thought about that. Once we get back to Sanford, I thought we three could jump into my car, come back to Bridlington and pick her up.'

'Yeah, but your car's a muck heap, Uncle Joe,' Lee pointed out. 'You never wash it and you don't have it validated.'

'You mean valeted,' Joe corrected his nephew. 'I've always said, it goes just as fast with the muck on it.'

'Borrow ours,' Cheryl suggested. 'It's bigger than Sheila's or Brenda's and cleaner than yours.'

Joe grunted a tacit agreement.

When the meal was over, while Lee and Cheryl took a tired Danny back to their room, Joe's two friends refused to wait any longer, and over drinks in the hotel bar, Joe told them everything that had happened since he left them on the promenade.

'The way I twigged the mugging was down to you, Brenda,' he explained. 'You were on about how big the cliffs at Flamborough were and how small they looked on your video. That's when it dawned on me that whoever attacked Angie on Friday night was way too tall to be Jess Collier.'

'So you're saying it had to be one of the Bulls?' Sheila demanded.

'Can you think of anyone else? A local scrote, maybe, but then you have to ask how did Jess end up with the bag. She knows the players, she was familiar with the players, she had to have taken it from one of them, and the favourites are Drummond and Grainger.'

'And you haven't tackled them?' Brenda demanded.

'Haven't even seen them this morning. And anyway, you know what happened last night.'

Brenda took his hand. 'Don't worry, Joe. I'll be with you and they won't dare take me on.'

Joe snorted. 'As if I need you. No, honest,

Brenda. You didn't see the state Angie was in. I did, and right now I'm so mad I'd be willing to take the SAS on.'

'And the initials in her phone contacts?' Sheila asked. 'You can't tie them to the Bulls?'

'Didn't I say so?'

'But you don't think he was the one who smashed her?' Brenda demanded.

'No. I don't. Even if they were at the end of their affair, I can't see any bloke doing that. I've explained my thinking on it. It's down to the Bulls players.'

It was obvious to them that he was getting angry, and in an effort to sidetrack the debate, Brenda asked, 'Are we any further forward on the Sanfordnatter business?'

'To be honest, I'd forgotten all about it. I haven't had any more complaints so whether Gemma's done something, I don't know.'

'Well, let's find out then.'

Before anyone could protest that it was Easter Sunday and Gemma would not take kindly to being disturbed, Brenda accessed her phone, and with a speed and accuracy Joe envied, went online to the Sanfordnatter page, and tried to log into the thread which had been so abusive.

She smiled at her friends. 'Nothing. The account's been closed.'

Joe wiped imaginary sweat from his brow. 'That has to be Gemma. And with it out of the way, we can concentrate on what's been going on here.'

'I disagree,' Sheila said. 'The state you were in last night, Joe, I think we should just leave it to the police.'

'Yes, well, like I say, you didn't see Angie. If you had, you might feel a bit different.'

Brenda finished her Campari, and stood up. 'I think what we need is a bit of a stress buster.'

Joe pointed at her empty glass. 'You've just had one.'

She tutted. 'I mean a bit of us time. What say we take a walk to the prom, and sit and look at the sea for a while?'

Sheila got to her feet. 'I think that's a sensible idea, Brenda. Come on, Joe. Finish your beer, and let's make a move.'

Joe was too old a hand not to know when he was beaten. He drained his glass of bitter, and followed them out into the pale, afternoon sunshine.

Five minutes later, they took a bench on the promenade, and looked out over the choppy, North Sea. It had the necessary calming effect, but it also energised memories of past 3rd Age Club excursions.

'I think this coast is bad news for us,' Sheila announced. 'Every time we come to this area, something goes wrong. Filey, Whitby twice, Scarborough, and now Bridlington.'

Brenda chuckled. 'I don't know about Scarborough. I mean, Joe got up close and cosy with Sandra Peagram, didn't he?'

'It's my magnetic personality,' Joe quipped.

'You still see her, Joe?' Sheila asked.

'Not for a while now. New Year was the last time I was over there, if you remember.'

Silence fell while they watched the Yorkshire

Belle making her way towards Flamborough Head once again.

It was Brenda who broke it. 'Poor Angela. I don't care who she's involved with, she doesn't deserve that.'

It reminded Joe of his annoyance. 'Nobody does. And that reminds me, I need a word with George Robson. The whisper is that he was over friendly with her at one bit.'

'I thought we came out to forget our troubles,' Sheila reminded them.

'That'll be the day,' Brenda announced.

A further twenty minutes passed, their conversation generalised, reflecting on the weekend, comparing it to other club excursions, and with the time coming up to half past three, Brenda checked her watch and said, 'We've had our half hour out, and I think it's time I was getting some sleep. This time tomorrow, we'll be home, and as it's the last night tonight, I intend making a night of it.' Quite abruptly, she changed the subject. 'You'll be talking to the members later, Joe?'

'Les suggested just before or just after dinner. Trouble is, I don't know what I can tell them. Freya Elliman said she'd ring me and let me know but I haven't heard anything yet.'

'Well, if nothing else, it's the ideal time to collar George Robson and see what he can tell you,' Sheila reminded him. 'Come on then. Time for thirty winks.'

Brenda laughed. 'Forty winks.'

'I was doing a Joe and saving ten winks for later.'

Having silently agreed with Brenda's suggestion of an afternoon nap, it was turned six o'clock when Joe woke up. He showered, shaved, and dressed for the evening. Once ready, he rang Freya for an update on Angela's condition.

'She should be back with you in the next few hours. Once they're happy that she can cope. No broken bones, no really serious injuries, but she'll be wearing a lot of make-up for the next few weeks.'

'If the hospital ring us here, we'll go for her,' Joe promised.

'No need. We'll bring her once we've taken a formal statement. Are you any further forward on identifying the culprit?'

'No. Angie hasn't told you anything?'

'I haven't spoken to her, but the officer we sent down to the urgent treatment centre, says Angela insists that she can't identify her attacker. I'll be honest, Joe, she had to be facing him so she must know who it is, and if she doesn't tell us, she could be guilty of withholding evidence.'

Joe sighed. 'I'll have a word with the girls, Sheila and Brenda. We've already agreed to get her home to Sanford by car, so we'll see if they can persuade her otherwise. I'll keep you posted.'

'Good enough,' Freya agreed. 'I'll probably see you later this evening.'

He arrived in the foyer at 7:15, and unwilling to put the club members off their evening meal, he deferred reporting to them until after dinner.

Consequently, at a few minutes to eight, he gathered them in a corner of the lounge, and gave them a succinct account of Angela's attack and her current situation.

'Sheila, Brenda, and I have agreed that Angie is unlikely to be fit enough to travel home by bus tomorrow, so once we're back in Sanford, we'll come straight back to Bridlington to collect her by car. I want to wrap this up by reminding you that she's a club member, and as such, she is entitled to our support, so please, treat her gently as and when she gets back here, don't press her too hard, but do give her whatever assistance you can. Thanks all of you.'

The brief meeting broke up with a rhubarb murmur of general conversation, other members began to spread themselves around the room, ready for Rita Penney's final appearance of the weekend.

Joe, Sheila, and Brenda chose a table near the exit, ready to welcome Angela when the police returned her to the hotel. They'd been sat there some five minutes when Ollister stood over them.

'Right, Joe, you said you needed a word with Drummond, and he's in the foyer. I'll be with you to make sure he answers your questions this time.'

Joe got to his feet. 'Good enough for me, Ollie.' He threw a tenner on the table. 'Get another round of drinks when you're ready,' he said to the two women. 'This won't take long.'

The fire of anger burning in him, Joe accompanied Ollister from the lounge to a discreet corner of the foyer where Drummond sat, his face set in a mask of thunder.

When they arrived, the young player half stood. 'I'm sick of telling you—'

Joe cut him off. 'Sit down, shut your mouth and open your ears.'

Drummond looked to Ollister, then Joe, then back at Ollister.

'Do it,' his chairman ordered.

Drummond acquiesced and Joe went on the attack. 'I got your brother out of the poop in Windermere, and I've tried to get you out of it since Friday, you idiot. All you ever had to do was speak to me. I know for a fact that you weren't in the Rising Sun with Jess Collier last Tuesday. From that point of view, I could have saved your marriage, but I don't know that you weren't with her on Friday here in Bridlington.'

'I've had nothing to do with Jess Collier for years. Not since I got engaged to Tilly, and I wasn't with her on Friday afternoon.'

'You were on Friday morning,' Joe challenged.

'At your place you mean? Yeah, so what? So was Niall Semple, and Ian Grainger. You saw all of us. Yes, and she was with Grainger on Friday afternoon when we got here. Knowing him, he was probably giving her what for in her room. And it's ten to one that he persuaded her to mug Angie Foster.'

A slow thread of realisation began to permeate Joe's mind. 'Persuade her to mug Angie? Why?'

Reluctant to answer, Drummond looked to Ollister. 'It's not my place to say anything.'

His boss was not willing to let it go. 'Get it said, Dave. Listen, lad, whether you know it or not, you're in the frame for killing Jess and knocking seven colours out of Angie Foster.'

'It wasn't me.'

'Then what did you mean when you said he might have persuaded Jess to rob Angie?' Joe demanded.

A beaten man, Drummond looked down on his hands, then around the room, before finally focusing on Joe. 'He's broke. He's been struggling for money for yonks. It's different for most of us. We play for the Bulls, and most of us, me included, have full-time jobs. Hell, I work for Ollie, don't I? Grainger doesn't have anything other than the few quid he makes on the field. Listen, Mr Murray, I can't swear to this, but I'm certain he goes out on the rob three or four nights a week.'

Joe looked to Ollister. 'Your nicked trophies, Angie's mugging? We need to pull Grainger.' He swung his attention back to Drummond. 'Everything you've told me, you'll have to say to the cops.'

'Hang on. I don't know about that.'

'Listen, you idiot, you are in the frame. You and Grainger. Are you willing to go down for the next fifteen or twenty years to protect him?'

Drummond's defeat was total. 'I'll tell them then. But it's only speculation. I mean, for all I know Ian could be borrowing money.'

Joe got to his feet. 'Talk to the cops. I'll leave him with you, Ollie. Let you give him the good news.'

'Good news?' Drummond asked. 'What good news?'

211

Ollister chuckled. 'You think they might let him go home, Joe?'

'Once he's given them a statement, yes. Have you any idea where we might find Grainger?'

'Not the foggiest. I don't know where any of them are except Roger, our coach. He's gone over to see that lass of yours. That Foster woman.'

And with those final words, the penny dropped for Joe. 'CS,' he muttered to himself. 'Coach Semple.'

Chapter Twenty

Leaving his friends in the bar watching Rita Penney, stepping outside for a smoke, Joe first rang Freya, and learned that the police had spoken to both Angela and Roger Semple, and although Angela denied that Roger had attacked her, he insisted that he had. He was charged with assault, and the inspector was in the process of arranging for a car to bring them both to the hotel. There was no mention of the killing of Jess Collier.

Joe was not fooled. He knew as well as Angela that Roger had not attacked her and his knowledge stemmed from one simple outburst.

But where was he? Having killed Jess Collier – probably by accident – and then later assaulted Angela, was he on the verge of doing something stupid?

Joe's watch read 8:45, and a glance across at the promenade said that night had closed in. The sea would be a black mass. The perfect setting for suicide.

With the feeling that this was a hopeless quest, Joe hurried from the smoke shelter, across to the promenade, looked both ways, and spotted him sitting on the same bench Joe and his two friends had occupied during the afternoon.

He strolled to the bench, sat down, spent a moment rolling another cigarette, and as he lit it he asked, 'All right, Niall?'

The young fullback turned a scowl on Joe. 'Do

us a favour and clear off.'

'Well, you see, lad, I can't do that. Not that I'm gonna grab you by the scruff of the neck and take you in.' Joe chuckled. 'I'm not big enough to do that. No, Niall, I'm thinking more about your dad than you.'

'My dad?'

'Yes. I was talking to the cops about ten minutes ago and your dad's confessed to battering Angie Foster. You're gonna let him take the fall, are you?'

Niall's shoulders slumped. 'The bloody idiot. Why did he do that?'

'I assume it's because he loves his son, and I imagine there'll be a fair bit of guilt over his affair with Angie.' Joe took a drag on his cigarette and let the smoke out with a loud hiss. 'Why don't you tell me how it all came about? Your dad and Angie, Jess Collier, everything.'

There was a long moment of silence while Niall stared out across the black sea.

'Things aren't good between Mam and Dad. They haven't been for yonks. Dad wants a divorce, Mam wants to try again. Then Dad took up with the Foster tart. I've been pleading with him for weeks to stop it, go back to Mam, but he doesn't want to know.'

'It must be difficult for you. I'm divorced. Have been for years, but we had no children and there was no one else involved in the split between me and my ex-wife. How did Jess Collier fit into this?'

'She was with Grainger on Friday afternoon.

He mugged the Foster woman for her handbag and then sent Jess out to try and sell it on. He had a contact or summat here in Bridlington, but when you intervened and called the cops, he daren't go himself. I saw her leave the hotel, followed her, got her down to the beach where we wouldn't be seen, and asked if I could just have a look through the bag, find anything that would let me put pressure on Foster, get her to back off from Dad. The silly cow told me to sod off and tried to walk away from me. I grabbed her scarf, dragged her back and she fell. Cracked her head on the stone sea wall. I panicked, man. I didn't know what do so I legged it. I didn't realise she was dead until the filth turned up on Friday night, and when they accused Foster, I thought, yeah, perfect. That'll get her claws out of Dad.'

Joe took another drag on his cigarette. 'I can see what you're saying, but it doesn't work like that, Niall. See, chances are that when they charge your old man for knuckling Angie, they'll bring up Jess's death, and if he knows what I know – and I'm betting he does – he'll confess to that too. Anything to save you going down. So, you've told me about Jess. What happened with Angie?'

Once again there was a moment of silence before Niall replied. 'Dad and her were getting it on early this afternoon. I was hanging about the second floor. Our room's on the same floor, mine and Grainger's. Two minutes after Dad left her, I knocked on the door. Obviously, she was expecting him, but when she opened the door, I pushed her back inside. There was a bit of an argument during

215

which I told her to keep away from my old man. She landed out at me, and I reacted. Punched her in the face. From there, I just lost it and battered the hell out of her. And then, all of a sudden, I came to my senses and I was terrified that I'd killed her too, so I ran for it.'

It did not take much for Joe to put the rest of it together. 'Your dad must have realised all this, knew that it was you, and decided that he was gonna take the rap. What you have to decide, Niall, is whether you're going to let him take that rap.'

Tears welled in the young man's eyes. 'What will I get?'

Joe decided there was no point trying to pull the wool over his eyes. 'It'll be prison, for sure. It sounds to me like Jess's death is manslaughter, and Angie's is a case of assault, maybe GBH. The courts will take into account your emotional state, your concerns for your parents and their marriage, but even so, they will wall you up for a while. But think about this, Niall. The same applies to your father. If you don't go down, he will.' Joe crushed out his cigarette on the ground, picked up the dead stub, and stood up. 'According to the cops, your dad and Angie will be back in the hotel very soon, so I'll leave you to think about it.'

Niall heaved in a huge breath and also got to his feet. 'There's nothing to think about, Mr Murray. I can't let Dad pay the price for me losing control.'

* * *

Monday morning dawned gloomy and threatening rain, but it was not only the weather depressing the mood at the breakfast table.

The police had arrested Niall Semple the previous evening, and based on Dave Drummond's statement, they took Ian Grainger in for questioning on the mugging of Angela Foster. Freya rang Joe at eight in the morning, saying they had charged him too, not only with stealing Angela's handbag but also with the theft of trophies from the Sanford Bulls' boardroom.

But not everyone was happy. As Joe, Sheila and Brenda took their morning meal, they learned that Roger Semple and Angela Foster were annoyed at the outcome.

As he arrived for breakfast, Semple stopped by their table and challenged Joe, 'Why don't you mind your own bloody business?'

'And let you go down for your son's crimes?'

'I had it arranged with Angie. She would drop the charges. And what crimes? He was concerned for his mother.'

'Killing Jess Collier isn't a crime?'

'It was an accident, man.'

At that point, Sheila stepped in. 'According to the account Niall gave Joe, it was manslaughter, Mr Semple, and that is a crime.'

Brenda, too, spoke up. 'And if you stuck to sleeping in your own bed, none of it would have happened.'

'That's smart coming from a woman with your reputation.'

Brenda was about to rise to the insult, but Joe

217

stayed her. 'Forget it, Brenda. You can't argue with idiocy.'

Semple glowered. 'You just keep your distance from me, Murray. That's all.' And with that, he stormed off.

Minutes later, Angela, her face still bruised and puffed up in places, arrived, and she sat with them, but she was not joining them.

'I have cause to thank you for your help this weekend, but even so, I'm a bit put out by the way you pressured young Niall into confessing last night.'

'Joe was keeping your lover out of the nick,' Brenda retorted.

Angela turned a half closed, sour eye on Brenda. 'Lover? What we had, Brenda, was occasional encounters, when we felt like it. And before Niall turned up in my room yesterday afternoon, Roger and I had already decided to end it. He's going to make an effort to get back with his wife. And if you hadn't twisted Niall's arm, it would all have ended peacefully.'

'Would it?' Joe demanded. 'What about that young woman who lost her life? That can be swept under the carpet, can it? As long as Roger and Niall Semple are happy, and you've had your bit of fun, Jess Collier doesn't matter?'

Angela squirmed. 'As of now, I'm quitting the 3rd Age Club. And you don't have to worry about getting me back to Sanford, Joe.' She stood up. 'Thanks to you there are vacant seats on the Sanford Bulls' bus, and Roger's going to arrange for me to go home with them.'

'And good bloody riddance,' Joe called to her back.

'Calm down, Joe,' Sheila advised. 'You can't always keep everyone happy.'

'And you did make two hundred pounds off Ollister, didn't you?' Brenda reminded him.

Almost on cue, Ollister appeared and hovered over them. 'All I can say, Joe, is I wish I'd never hired you.'

'And that would have saved Jess Collier's life would it?' Joe demanded. 'It would have stopped Grainger's thieving? It would have saved Angie Foster from a good hiding? I'll send you my bill, Ollie, but do me a favour. If you need a private eye, don't bother ringing.'

Ollister might have responded but Sheila got in first. 'Did Tilly and Dave make it up?'

'I think so. He was on his way home last night after he'd spoken to the police. Oh, and the baby was a girl.'

'Well, congratulations, grandad,' Brenda said and Sheila murmured her agreement.

Ollister wandered off and Joe asked, 'Is it have a go at Joe day today?'

Before either of the women could reply, his phone rang. 'Gemma,' he said after checking the menu.

He made the connection and listened, making only the occasional comments. Eventually, he thanked his niece and ended the call.

'Well?' Sheila asked.

'They managed to get the Sanfordnatter account shut down – as we know – but they can't get any handle on the guy what set it up. Apparently, his name is My Lastlaff and he lives at my address.'

The women tittered.

'Never mind, Joe,' Brenda chuckled. 'At least you've got me back to something like normal.'

Joe drank his coffee. 'Just don't ask me to consider Bridlington again, I told you we should have gone to Benidorm.'

At that moment, Lee hurried over, his face a mask of worry.

'What's up, lad?' Joe asked.

'It's Cheryl, Uncle Joe. She's been sick again. She thinks she's pregnant.'

'Oh, well done, Lee,' Brenda cheered.

'Congratulations, Lee,' Sheila echoed, 'but why the concerned face?'

'I can't think what's caused it.'

Joe groaned. 'I need another life.'

THE END

THANK YOU FOR READING. I HOPE YOU HAVE ENJOYED THIS BOOK. WOULD YOU BE KIND ENOUGH TO LEAVE A RATING OR REVIEW ON AMAZON?

The Author

David W Robinson retired from the rat race after the other rats objected to his participation, and he now lives with his long-suffering wife in sight of the Pennine Moors outside Manchester.

Best known as the creator of the light-hearted and ever-popular **Sanford 3rd Age Club Mysteries**, **Mrs Capper's Casebooks** and in a similar vein the Spookies Paranormal Mysteries. He also produces darker, more psychological crime thrillers as in the **Feyer & Drake** thrillers and occasional standalone titles sometimes under the pen name **Robert Devine**

He produces his own videos, and can frequently be heard grumbling against the world on Facebook at https://www.facebook.com/dwrobinsonauthor where you're more than welcome to **follow me and my work**.

He has a YouTube channel at https://www.youtube.com/user/Dwrob96/videos. For more information you can track him down at www.dwrob.com and if you want to sign up to my newsletter and pick up a **#FREE book or two**, you can find all the details at https://dwrob.com/readers-club/

All books by David W Robinson

The Sanford 3rd Age Club Mysteries
The Filey Connection
The I-spy Murders
A Halloween Homicide
A Murder for Christmas
Murder at the Murder Mystery Weekend
My Deadly Valentine
The Chocolate Egg Murders
The Summer Wedding Murder
Costa del Murder
Christmas Crackers
Death in Distribution
A Theatrical Murder
Killing in the Family
Trial by Fire
Peril in Palmanova
The Squire's Lodge Murders
Murder on the Treasure Hunt
A Cornish Killing
Merry Murders Everyone
A Tangle in Tenerife
Tis the Season to be Murdered
Confusion in Cleethorpes
Murder on the Movie Set:
A Deadly Twixmas
Naked Murder
Murder at the Christmas Meddlercon

Missing with Menaces
Bridlington Bedlam

Special Editions
Tales from the Lazy Luncheonette Casebook
Boxed Set #1

Mrs Capper's Casebooks
Mrs Capper's Christmas
Death at the Wool Fair
Blackmail at the Ballot Box:
Exit Page Ten:
A Professional Dilemma
Murder at Christmas Manor
A Call to Murder
Death of Innocence
Death at the Diet Club
The Christmas Festival Murder
A Quizzical Drowning
Scarborough Not Fair
A Cryptic Christmas Cat-Nabbing

The Midthorpe Mysteries
A case of Missing on Midthorpe
A case of Bloodshed in Benidorm

SPOOKIES Paranormal Mysteries
The Haunting of Melmerby Manor
The Man in Black

Feyer & Drake
The Anagramist
The Frame
I C Crypt

Thrillers written as Robert Devine
Dominus
The Power
Kracht
The Cutter (Published by Bloodhound Books)

LOOKING FOR A COUPLE OF FREEBIES?

Then why not sign up to my newsletter. I guarantee you will not be spammed and I'm not in the business of selling email address. You'll receive not more than two or three emails per month, but best of all when you sign up to, you'll be guided to a page where you can download not one but TWO FREE BOOKS.

Visit https://dwrob.com/readers-club/ for details.

Do you want to know where I'm up at any given time? Then why not follow me on Facebook?

You have the following options. Follow me on my Facebook author page or you can join reader groups at David W Robinson & Readers and Ex DSK Crime Writers or you can do all three.

I welcome comments and feedback on both Amazon and Facebook.

Go on. You know you want to.

Printed in Dunstable, United Kingdom